COMPASS IN THE
BLOOD

COMPASS IN THE BLOOD

BY WILLIAM E. COLES JR.

Atheneum Books for Young Readers
New York London Toronto Sydney Singapore

Atheneum Books for Young Readers
An imprint of Simon & Schuster Children's Publishing Division
1230 Avenue of the Americas
New York, New York 10020

Book design by Sonia Chaghatzbanian
The text of this book is set in Matrix.

Printed in the United States of America

10 9 8 7 6 5 4 3 2 1

Library of Congress Cataloging-in-Publication Data
Coles, William E. Jr.
Compass in the blood / William E. Coles Jr.—1st ed.
p. cm.
Summary: While working with a Pittsburgh television journalist on a
project to uncover the truth about the 1902 Katherine Soffel scandal,
college student Dee Armstrong learns about different types of loyalty
and betrayal.
ISBN 0-689-83181-1
[1. Betrayal—Fiction. 2. Soffel, Katherine, 1867–1909—Fiction.
3. Pittsburgh (Pa.)—Fiction. 4. Mystery and detective stories.] I. Title.
PZ7.C67746 Sf 2001
[Fic]   00-028875

FIRST EDITION

For Jan
The One and Only

Our forefathers could drive their oxen
through the dangerous mountain valleys.
They could shield their families from savages,
knew how to deal with the wild and strange,
had the points of the compass in their blood.

They knew the mountains and the midnight skies.
We know chambers filled with talk and silence,
ghosts and hallucinations.

Our fathers died victorious over the outward.
Peace to them. Courage to us,
who fight not Indians but insanity.

Living rooms, bedrooms, court-houses,
banks, asylums,
are no more mysterious than the out of doors;
we shall know them and ourselves who dwell in them,
and what the shapes that dwell in the wilderness
within us all.

We have senses which may lead to trails,
we may find trails which lead to water;
we are making a new compass
from the compasses of yesterday;
even in the fantastic air of chambers,
are feeling our way towards passes through the mountains.

Our forefathers went shadowlike
into beautiful dangerous new valleys.
We are their children; we too explore and hope,
making the filaments of a new compass
out of our need to come to terms with ourselves,
with the others who live life with us,
and the life that lives all.

Haniel Long
From "Prologue," *Pittsburgh Memoranda,* 1935

CHAPTER I

D ee's roommate and best friend, Megan, had left
the note on the table just inside the front door
of their apartment. It was a typical Megan message,
information with an attitude:

Dee glanced quickly at her watch on the way
across the room to the telephone—5:15—and then, without even taking off her backpack and parka, began
dialing. She noticed her hands were shaking.

She heard a buzz and a click, then "WHGH Radio
and TV."

Dee blurted out the extension number, and someone answered almost immediately.

"Harry Bromfield's office. Judy Barronger speaking."

"Yes . . . Hi. I was supposed to call about a meeting? I mean, someone . . . I think you, called about my
arranging a meeting with . . . with Ms. Bromfield?"

"And to whom am I speaking, please?"

"Oh, right," Dee said with a nervous little laugh.
She put her hand on her chest. "Diane Armstrong? I'm
a freshman at the University of Pittsburgh, and my
roommate left a message—"

"Yes, of course, Ms. Armstrong," the secretary interrupted smoothly. "Now, today is Wednesday . . ."
Dee heard some pages being turned. "Would it be
convenient for you to meet with Ms. Bromfield
here, in her office, for a conversation, say, . . .
could you possibly do it tomorrow, at about two in
the afternoon? That would be Thursday, February
nineteenth."

"Sure," Dee said quickly. "I mean, tomorrow's fine."
Ordinarily on Thursday afternoons and two other afternoons of the week, she waitressed at Bagelnosh, but
she could easily get someone to fill in for her.

"And you know where we are? On Fifth Avenue just
down from Pitt?"

"Oh, yeah, I know where the station is."

"Good. We'll call it firm, then. We're on the second
floor, room two four seven. Just ask at the information

desk how to get to Ms. Bromfield's office and tell them you're expected."

Dee thanked her and hung up. The whole exchange hadn't taken two minutes.

"Yes!" she said out loud, bringing both fists down in front of her as if pounding on a table. Then, shrugging off her backpack, she sat on the edge of the couch to catch up with herself.

Harriet Bromfield, or Harry, as she liked to be known, Pittsburgh's most flamboyant and controversial TV journalist, had been a hero for Dee ever since high school. She'd started to make a name for herself with her documentary films on women: Susan B. Anthony; Harriet Tubman; "Mother" Ann Lee, the founder of the Shakers in the United States. But it was her film last fall on Katherine Soffel, Pittsburgh's most notorious female criminal and center of the most sensational love affair ever to have rocked the city, that had made Dee decide to try to get in touch with Harry. The self-confidence with which the production took charge of the Soffel story by going straight to the core of it, Harry's control of her subject, as though she were a playwright creating characters—these things had dazzled Dee, the more so because she herself, just a few months earlier, had written a prize-winning senior term paper on the local newspapers' outrageously prejudiced coverage of the case at the time.

Thorough as Dee believed her own research had

been, the film made use of things she didn't know and also suggested interpretations of the case she hadn't even imagined. She'd written to Harry excitedly, praising her work and asking several questions about sources; impulsively, she'd also enclosed a copy of the prize-winning paper. But there had been no reply. Until now, that is.

What could Harry possibly want to see her about five months later? Why hadn't Dee at least thought to ask Judy what's-her-name a couple of questions?

Still absorbed in thought, she got up, went into her bedroom, and dropped her parka onto the unmade bed. She kicked her work boots into a corner, slid out of her jeans and sweater, and into a sweat suit—one of three she owned, all of them oversized and as soft and comforting as the stuffed animals of her childhood.

Then it struck her that she'd been seeing tomorrow's meeting as an interview when all the journalist really wanted, most likely, was to be nice to the high school kid who'd sent her her term paper.

Dee went into the kitchen, then back to her bedroom, and finally into the bathroom, where she stared at herself in the mirror.

If Harry were only doing her PR duty, though, she could have done it with just a phone call or a note months ago. This meeting *had* to be an interview of some sort. Maybe Harry had liked Dee's research on Mrs. Soffel and was considering using her on some other project. But in that case, maybe the fact that she hadn't asked the secretary any questions, that she'd just agreed meekly to trot down to the station the very next day, would be seen as unprofessional and count against her.

She walked back into the tiny living room and looked at the clock on the bookcase. It was only 5:40. Her boyfriend, Cory, usually slept for an hour or so after he finished work at 5:00, and getting him on the phone where he lived was impossible. Megan wouldn't be back from her job waitressing until after 8:00, and she wasn't exactly a fan of Harry's anyway. Once, she and Dee had watched the journalist, as a member of a local talk show panel, take on an unfriendly critic by leading him into pronouncements that at first she pretended to be intimidated by but then coolly destroyed. "Jeez," Megan had said, "that lady's a real killer. She waits and then jumps just like a spider." And from that had come the nickname Spider Woman, or sometimes Spider Lady.

Feeling she'd explode if she didn't talk to someone, Dee decided to call Carol Muskowitz about filling in for her at Bagelnosh.

"Hey," Carol said. "You got it. I can use the money."

"I wouldn't ask you on such short notice," Dee couldn't resist saying, "but I just got a call to come talk to Harry Bromfield."

"Get out!" Carol exclaimed. "The TV lady?"

"Yeah," Dee said nonchalantly. "We may be doing some work together."

After talking with Carol, Dee just sat for a moment. Then she went back into her bedroom, opened her closet, and began laying clothes on her bed. Something mature was what she wanted, as close as she could get to what women executives wore in the ads on CNN. She had only two long skirts, one tan, one blue. The blue it would be; she had blue shoes and panty hose. All she needed was a dressy top like one of Megan's tailored silk blouses, which Dee knew she could borrow.

Okay. Now, what else?

The Soffel case.

She'd better have all the details of it—and more importantly, all the details of Harry's documentary— freshly in mind. She got both the paper she'd written almost a year ago and her video of Harry's film out of her bottom desk drawer, made a cup of Celestial Seasonings Mint Magic tea, and then stretched out on the living room couch to reread what she'd written.

Her paper had originally been written simply to fulfill a graduation requirement, not because she was either a history or a crime buff, and certainly not with the intention of competing for a prize. In fact, she wasn't completely sure why the Soffel case had fascinated her so much. She was aware, of course, that her interest in it coincided with her parents' sudden divorce that same winter and with Cory's coming into her life a little bit later, but the connections were vague to her and not something she liked thinking about anyway. All she knew for certain was that it mattered to her who Kate Soffel really was and why she'd done what she'd done. Dee had read everything she could find on the case in the Carnegie Library, and for the first time in her life she found herself rewriting something she'd written for a school project, and then rewriting that. The paper was still a source of pride to her.

As soon as she'd finished rereading her work, Dee slid the video of Harry's film into her VCR and settled back on the couch to watch. It was going to be no less than the fifth or sixth time she'd seen it.

CHAPTER 2

The Kate Soffel scandal in Pittsburgh at the beginning of the twentieth century had been written up in newspapers all over the world, and no wonder. It was an adulterous love story with everything, including millennial reverberations. Indeed, perhaps one of the main reasons the story had been told and retold for almost a hundred years was its prophetic quality—though what exactly was being prophesied was not always agreed upon.

The main elements of the scandal, incredible as they may have been, did not seem in question. The year was 1902. Katherine Soffel was the wife of the warden of Allegheny County Jail in downtown Pittsburgh, where they lived with their four young children in a special section of the jail designed as the warden's residence. Kate was high-strung and sensitive, but by all accounts a good wife and mother, civic-minded, a devout member of the Smithfield Evangelical Church. It was her custom to do what she could to ease the prisoners' lots by offering them spiritual comfort along with small gifts of tobacco and the like, and it was this that had led to the tragedy.

Kate sought to console two young prisoners who were awaiting execution for murder, the Biddle brothers, by reading the Bible to them through the bars of their cells. But, the story was, she became attracted to one of them, the handsome and dashing Ed Biddle, almost ten years younger than she, and not only let herself be talked into smuggling in the saws and guns the brothers needed to break out of jail, but insisted that they take her with them on their flight to freedom.

In less than thirty-six hours the three fugitives were tracked down in their stolen horse-drawn sleigh. As the posse approached, Ed Biddle, at Kate's insistence, shot her in the chest. The brothers then gave themselves mortal wounds, though the posse riddled their bodies with bullets for good measure as they lay in the snow. Miraculously, Kate recovered, but she was sent to Western Pennsylvania Penitentiary, and not long after, her husband divorced her for adultery. She was released after serving about two

9

years and went to live under an assumed name on Pittsburgh's North Side, where she worked as a dressmaker until her death six years later. It was generally believed that she never saw her children again.

Harry's documentary, *The Kate Soffel Affair: Some Unanswered Questions,* provoked the same sort of controversy her earlier work had. All the critics conceded that the film showed she had a wonderful eye for contrasts and camera angles and an ability to bring the ordinary together with the bizarre in a way that could be truly arresting. But what for some was a "brilliantly interpretive rendering of history" for others was "glib sensationalism," no more than "a self-promoting game being played at history's expense."

The production challenged the telling of Katherine Soffel's story as a love story—either the sort that made her into a pathetic romantic fool or one that represented her as a tragic heroine, bravely choosing to endure the world's scorn to follow the dictates of her heart.

It opened with a shot of Harry seated quietly behind a desk in front of a towering wall of books. Her long dark hair hung straight and glossy to just below her shoulders. She had on hoop earrings and a pair of enormous tinted glasses that made her look smart and sexy at the same time. She rose and glided around her desk to half sit on the front of it, one elegantly booted leg hanging free. "Good evening," she said in her low, full voice, a voice that Dee would have killed to have for herself. "Our subject tonight is a Pittsburgh woman, one who lived and who suffered and died here almost a hundred years ago. Her name is Kate Soffel, Katherine Dietrich Soffel, the most notorious scarlet woman our city has ever produced. *This* lady—"

The photograph that filled the screen had brought Dee forward in her seat the first time she'd seen it. It was a picture of a very regal-looking, dark-haired woman with sad, compassionate eyes. Katherine Soffel, obviously, but where had Harry found it?

"Or," Harry's voice continued, "was this Kate Soffel?"

And then the screen filled with a second photograph, one that Dee knew well from her research. It was the portrait of Kate Soffel all the Pittsburgh newspapers had used in 1902, and, as was clear when the two pictures were shown side by side, it was a retouched version of the first. The retouching, though, had turned an attractive woman of thirty-four, Kate's age when the Biddles escaped, into a heavily jowled matron of fifty, her mouth drooping with stupidity, eyes dead as stones.

"This revised Kate is the one the media offered the people of Pittsburgh together with a story about her that is as old as Adam and Eve, that is in fact a form of the Adam and Eve story."

The screen went black except for a white dot at

the center that began whirling and moving toward the viewer. It was the front page of a newspaper, the *Pittsburgh Post,* with a dateline of Friday morning, January 31, 1902. The camera then moved over the headlines:

ROMANTIC FOLLY OF WOMAN GAVE FREEDOM TO MURDEROUS BIDDLES

Cut Bars with Saws and Cowed Guards on Ranges with Revolvers Furnished by Warden's Wife

Story of Daring, Cunning, Infatuation

One of Three Custodians Beaten Insensible and All Locked in Dungeons
Mrs. Soffel May Have Gone with the Murderers
Escape Was a Complete Success

Warden Soffel Temporarily Suspended by Prison Board

"Now," Harry said, as a number of comparable headlines from the *Pittsburgh Leader,* the *Sun,* and the *Chronicle* flashed across the screen, "the thing to notice about such reporting is that all seven newspapers in Pittsburgh were telling the same story of what happened with the Biddles and Kate *less than twenty-four hours after the escape*—way before, that is, any kind of inquiry had established anything—and they were all telling the same story virtually the same way."

A black-and-white cartoon of a monster filled the screen, a female monster depicted as trampling four children in her slavering eagerness to enter a sewer. The drawing was rapidly followed by others rendering Kate in turn as a lustful-looking goat, a monkey, a vampire, and a gullible Eve accepting an apple from a two-headed snake labeled "The Biddles."

"Kate in this story is always an Eve figure, the Faithless Wife—either the scheming, cold-blooded accomplice of the Biddles from the beginning or a kind of crazy lady, weak-minded enough or sentimentally diseased enough or sexually depraved enough to have been seduced into becoming an accomplice. The Biddles"—a number of photographs and drawings of two sinisterly good-looking young men quickly replaced one another while Harry spoke over them—"are the wily agents of Satan, on the surface charming and spontaneous, vital, daring, erotically attractive, but underneath as diabolically evil, as subversive of law and order, as the snake in the Garden of Eden."

Harry paused a moment and then added, "Interestingly, the Biddles' role in the Adam and Eve version of

Kate's story is very much like that sometimes played today by black males in the bigoted mythology of white middle-class America, where they are imagined as the kinds of supercharged sexual machines that certain women are simply powerless to resist."

Dee shook her head, smiling in admiration. That was the sort of move in Harry's work she loved best, the quick illumination of the present through the past or vice versa; it was like the sounds of instruments coming together in the playing of a symphony.

"And finally," Harry went on, "there is this figure, Mr. Peter K. Soffel," and on the screen came a photo of a scrawny-necked official, pompous-looking, balding, his mouth totally obscured by a mustache that hung from under his nose like a curtain. "This is the third point of the eternal triangle, the cuckolded husband. But as a prison warden, Peter was also a guardian of civilization, of God's kingdom, and it is this as well as her home and children on which Kate was said to have turned her blasphemous back."

From there Harry proceeded to show how the story told about Kate Soffel and "the Biddle Boys," as they were called—a story told not just in Pittsburgh, but in newspapers throughout the world—was no more than a playing out of roles assigned them from the start. Lawlessness, after its brief dance in the sun, was stripped of its appeal and reduced by death and desolation to the shameful thing all decent people knew it to be. Thus conventional social values not only emerged alive and well, they emerged triumphant.

The camera returned to Harry, still half sitting on the front of her desk, head down, her free leg nodding slightly. Slowly she raised her head and smiled, very knowingly, but warmly too, as though to a small circle of friends. It hadn't been until Dee's second or third viewing of the film that she'd become aware she was smiling back at the screen. The woman really was magnetic.

"But there is another way of telling the story," Harry continued, "for which a different Kate is needed." Dee sat up and hunched herself forward with both forearms on her knees. What was coming was her favorite part.

The screen filled then with still another portrait photograph, one that had also been new to Dee. It was Kate at age nineteen, Harry's voice-over reported, and the picture had been taken just before her marriage. It was the face of a girl who looked as Dee had always imagined Joan of Arc; fiercely innocent, fiercely brave, and fiercely sad.

"For the story of *this* woman," Harry said, "let's listen to something published not at the time, but over thirty years later, once people had had the chance to consider some of the different things the Soffel case might mean."

Dee had not known who Haniel Long was, nor had she ever heard of the poem "Mrs. Soffel 1902" from his book *Pittsburgh Memoranda* published in 1935. But Harry's presentation of it had made such an impression on her last fall that she'd bought Long's book at the Pitt Bookstore the day after the documentary had aired.

"Friday, January thirty-first," the poem opened,

> *the Biddle brothers, Jack and Ed, escaped*
> *from murderers' row in the Allegheny County*
> *jail—the jail of Richardson romanesque,*
> *which makes downtown Pittsburgh even to the eye*
> *baronial, and brings back the dark strongholds*
> *and the dark sieges of feudalism, when likewise*
> *a baron was a baron.*

The boys' escape from the blackness of Pittsburgh, Long went on to say, was made possible by Mrs. Soffel, an "angel of light," he called her, who believed in their innocence and even petitioned the governor for mercy for them, "though she obviously did not expect him to show any." As the noose came nearer and nearer, hour by hour,

> *she read the Bible aloud*
> *to the Biddles, and they sawed through the bars of*
> *the cell.*

"With your love I can start over," Ed told her,
and she believed him. She had seen many prisoners,
but she believed Ed; her heart had given her orders.

The poem seemed to Dee absolutely made for Harry's style because so much of it was devoted to highlighting the bizarre elements in the public's responses:

when Mrs. Soffel
opened her eyes in the Butler jail, they told her
the boys were dead, and she said, "I am alone now."
It was no more than the truth. At the begrimed jail
in the heart of the town of Butler they charged admission
to see the bodies of the boys (an event of this kind
being a plain windfall to them, as indeed to us
O Pittsburghers, to-day and forever) and an attendant
kept bawling, "Gentlemen please remove their hats";
and when they closed the doors, they had to open them
again, because an aged man and a youth
had driven a long way to see the bodies, and ought to
be given a look. At Beinhauer's Funeral Parlor,
Pittsburgh, Southside, thousands of women fought
to see the dead boys, and the police had all they could do;
and a woman in deep mourning heaped evergreens
on the coffins, and it so displeased a relative of the
Biddles
that he ordered the doors closed.

Harry dramatized Long's emphasis on the startling contradictions of life in Pittsburgh by having different voices read sections of the poem behind photographs in which images of tremendous strength and vitality alternated with examples of preposterous affluence and unspeakable squalor. There was a picture of a printed menu for a nine-course dinner given at a Pittsburgh hotel, for instance, with oysters and squab and suckling pig, and then a quick cut to a heap of slaughtered chickens crawling with flies in the stall of an open market. There were pictures of open-hearth furnaces roaring with heat and of great cauldrons pouring out steel in rivers of light. There were shots of enormous machines, five stories high, ten stories high, at work gobbling up hillsides of slag and rock in order to create whole new landscapes. But then there were the jammed and dilapidated tenements of the immigrant mill workers, along with shots of their children playing barefoot in gutters that ran with filth. There was a grisly picture of a number of severed arms and legs piled like garbage into baskets at the rear of a hospital and, most unforgettably for Dee, a shot of a cat dangling from a clothesline in a tiny hangman's noose. And always there was the greasy smoke of the mills winding into schools and jails and mansions, slicking the rivers, holding the city even at noon as though deep inside a pocket. But the smoke was the sign and seal of a powerful new world as well, rising triumphant like a volcanic island from the sea.

The conclusion of Long's poem found in Mrs. Soffel's story "a manifestation Himalayan,"

> *reminding one there are hidden forces*
> *to renew life, make it a sudden marvel*
> *of poetry, music, madness for an enslaved city*
> *and a love-starved people: reminding one how little*
> *we know of love, how well it might be to know more.*

Harry accompanied Long's final words—"There is / Life within life and any appearance of it / a great and shining star in a black night"—with a series of photographs in which showers of sparks from smokestacks turned first into a peppering of stars and then into a great sprawling galaxy. Hokey maybe, but it worked.

Impressive as Harry made Long's story of Kate Soffel, however, it had never been the whole story for Dee—not any more than the glamorizing Hollywood film *Mrs. Soffel* had been. She couldn't forget those four small children Kate had deserted or her turning her back on her marriage, no matter how dull her domestic life might have been. But from the appearance of Cory in her own life not long after her mother and father had divorced, she could understand what it meant to say, as Long did, that the appearance of love in one's life is "a great and shining star in a black night."

The camera focused once more on Harry seated behind her desk. She smiled, rose, and, eyes downcast, again came round to perch on the front of the desk. Then, with a flip of her head that made her long dark hair ripple about her shoulders before falling perfectly back into place, she looked up and stared straight into the camera. The gesture was one of her trademarks; Dee had tried unsuccessfully a number of times to imitate it.

"But what if there were no romantic connection between Kate and Ed Biddle—as he in his dying confession swore there had not been, and as she in a signed confession made just after she'd been sentenced to prison swore as well?"

That reference to Kate's "signed confession" had startled Dee when she'd first heard it, and it was one of the things she'd asked Harry about in her unanswered letter. She knew that several confessions *supposedly* made by Kate had appeared in the newspapers, but all of them had been exposed as forgeries. Dee made a mental note to ask Harry again about the reference tomorrow.

"What if the *real* story of Kate Soffel and the Biddles," Harry continued, "involves an even deeper betrayal than that of adultery, and feelings much more complicated than those of simple sexual frustration and fulfillment?"

She folded her arms and stared with great earnestness directly into the camera. "What if no one in Pittsburgh—or anywhere else, for that matter—has even seen, let alone understood, Katherine Dietrich Soffel at all?"

At this point the television screen went black for a station break.

CHAPTER 3

The possibility of there being an untold story about Kate and the Biddles, Harry went on to explain after the break, depends on nothing more than how certain pieces of evidence are put together with certain other pieces of evidence.

There was the behavior of Warden Peter Soffel, Kate's supposedly loving husband, to consider, whose first statement when he was informed that the Biddles had escaped—and this was before Kate's involvement in the breakout had even been suggested—was that his wife must have chloroformed him. His first action was to order the Biddles' empty cells thoroughly cleaned and washed down and everything in them burned; his second was to gather up from his own residence all books, magazines, and papers belonging to Kate and burn them as well, in order, he explained later, that his children not be "contaminated by anything she may have been corrupted by."

Yet for the next several days, the more the warden was questioned, the more things he discovered that he'd evidently missed in his initial housecleaning. A love letter supposedly from Ed Biddle to Kate (in which she is asked to purchase some saws and revolvers) was found hidden under the carpet of her bedroom. Then the saws themselves were retrieved from the back of one of Kate's bureau drawers. From behind a screen came some torn up pieces of paper that, when smoothed out and pieced together, showed the code used by Kate and Ed to communicate with each other, even though they spoke in person daily. Five or six days after the escape, a second love letter from Ed Biddle showed up, this one mailed to the warden by a clairvoyant in nearby Allegheny City in whose parlor Kate was supposed to have dropped it.

And far from Kate's having established her relationship with the Biddles behind her husband's back, as he claimed, there was a lot of evidence that it was *his* idea that Kate visit the Biddles on death row in the first place—even though such visits, particularly when they were unsupervised, as Kate's had been, were in direct violation of prison regulations. Moreover, it was the warden who insisted that Kate continue her visits even after the newspapers had criticized him for allowing them.

Then, with the help of diagrams, Harry pointed out some very strange things about the escape itself. For instance, the only way out of the maximum-security area where the Biddles were imprisoned was through an iron door that could be opened only from the outside or with a key from within; it was strictly forbidden for that key to be brought into the prison proper under any circumstances. Yet the night of the escape one of the guards *did* bring in the key, which the Biddles stole when they overpowered him; otherwise, sawn bars and all, they would never have gotten any farther than the corridor outside their cells. Another odd thing was that though a new electric alarm system had recently been installed in the prison, and though all the guards had been made familiar with its operation, and though the button to set it off was conspicuous in the guardroom, not one of the three guards on duty the night the Biddles escaped even thought to use it.

And was it not puzzling, Harry asked, that the escape was so badly planned in a couple of very striking particulars, puzzling especially in light of the Biddles' expertise as criminals and the months they'd had as prisoners to think about what they were going to do? Why did they elect to leave the jail (let alone stop by the warden's residence to pick up Kate) on the coldest night of the coldest winter on Pittsburgh record without warm clothing (Kate was dressed as though for a party, in a long black dress and a fancy plumed hat), with no money, and with no more of a plan for getting out of the city in the middle of a predicted snowstorm than to walk from downtown out to the suburbs somewhere—this in spite of the fact that the Biddles had many friends in the city who would have hidden and helped them? And surely one of the boys would have realized, even if Kate hadn't, that to travel as a threesome was going to make them all that much easier to catch. Why hadn't they split up?

Harry went through each of the main events of the case in the same manner, raising question after question behind photograph after photograph of various features of the prison, of the fugitives' escape route through the city, of their various stopping points, of the Biddles' bullet-riddled bodies laid out at Beinhauer's Funeral Parlor, of Kate being carried from a sleigh, lying in the hospital, being escorted from the courthouse to begin serving her sentence.

It was not that Dee had never heard any of these questions raised before; indeed, many had appeared in the newspapers of the time, which she had read when she was researching her paper. But before watching Harry's documentary, Dee had never seen the questions put together so as to show just how many loose ends there were to whatever way one wanted to tell the story of Kate and the Biddles—either as an acting out of mental illness, or as a celebration of love's power and importance, or as some different kind of story altogether.

The *real* story of what had happened—that was what Harry called the key question; and her documentary offered several possible answers to it. Maybe Kate had engineered the Biddles' escape and her flight with them not only knowing they would all be caught, but *hoping* they would be so that the brothers' deaths (and possibly her own) might make some kind of political statement about the injustice of the legal system or the repression of women. Or maybe Kate engineered the escape out of hatred for her marriage and her husband, out of a desire to ruin and humiliate him.

Or perhaps there had been a conspiracy of some sort behind the Biddles' escape and Kate's part in it. Were there unidentified accomplices, such as some of the guards, one of whom was Kate's father? (He admitted to carrying messages between the Biddles and his daughter, though he claimed to be ignorant of their content.)

But what would have been the object of such a conspiracy? Could it have been political? A way of trying to discredit Warden Soffel as a Republican appointee and, through him, the Republican machine that was then running the city of Pittsburgh? Perhaps some of the guards had been bribed by the Democrats to let the Biddles go, and then, just to make sure that the escape doubly humiliated the warden, perhaps they had also coerced Kate into becoming involved by telling her that her help was the only chance there was to rectify a great injustice and that she as a "hostage" would be taken only a block or so and then let go while the Biddles were spirited away to Canada.

Still another possibility was that *both* Kate and the Biddles had been set up, the motive for which had nothing to do with politics, but rather with Peter Soffel's desire in one stroke to get himself out of a job he detested, rid of a wife he no longer loved, and to be made sole owner of his wife's property as well as sole custodian of their children. Was this the reason the Biddles had been shot into such conveniently silent pieces even after they'd already been disarmed and were obviously dying? No one except Kate's husband had been permitted to talk with her after her capture either, not for almost a week. And perhaps such a scenario was the best possible explanation of the strange disparity between what Kate freely admitted to in her comments on the escape and what she would say nothing about, between her full and reasonable explanations of some things and her garbled, virtually nonsensical accounts of others. (Here Harry drew heavily on the "signed confession" she had alluded to earlier.) Had Kate been silenced by someone, or by several someones, under threat that if she talked she would never see any of her children again?

"In May of 1902," Harry concluded her film by saying, "Kate was sentenced to serve two years in the penitentiary, and in December of 1903, her husband was granted a divorce for adultery without her being present in the courtroom. Shortly before the divorce was final, with time off for good behavior, Kate was released. She changed her name and, by design, sank into obscurity. In the summer of 1909, Kate was stricken with typhoid fever and lingered in the hospital for over a week without a single family member ever coming to visit her. She is buried in Smithfield Cemetery."

The film's final shot was of graves in a cemetery, row after row of them, their headstones weathered and lichen-covered. From there the camera panned up to a view of the downtown Pittsburgh skyline glowing enigmatically in the setting sun.

"Whatever really happened with Kate Soffel and the Biddles sleeps with her; for the most part, she remained silent about the most important event in her life. But it is difficult not to speculate on what she might have said had she had a voice of her own, and an audience she thought could hear it."

As the credits rolled up the screen, Dee found herself feeling the same sense of mystery she always experienced after seeing Harry's film. Who was Kate exactly? Why had she done what she had?

A verse Dee had come across somewhere during her research and memorized put it perfectly:

> *In leading them out of the Way of Sorrows*
> *In leading them under the Bridge of Sighs*
> *Her action still the question poses,*
> *What she revered and what defied.*
>
> *Was it all for love, or sickness rampant,*
> *Or something somewhere in between,*
> *That led this prison warden's wife*
> *To dream the act and act the dream?*

And tomorrow at 2:00 P.M., Dee was actually going to meet the woman who had done the most to make this mystery live for her.

CHAPTER 4

The moment after Judy buzzed through the announcement of Dee's arrival, the door of Harriet Bromfield's office burst open.

"Dee!" she called warmly as she came forward smiling with her hand extended. "How nice of you to come." The woman radiated energy. She had on the same large round glasses she wore on camera and the same type of hoop earrings, but she was shorter than Dee had expected, and older, forty maybe, though Dee had never been any good at guessing ages. Her expensive-looking paisley blouse, culottes, and high leather boots made Dee feel a little like a child dressed for church.

"It's good to meet you, Ms. Bromfield," Dee said, taking the extended hand. She almost expected to feel vibration, as with a heavy bass in a speaker.

"Harry, please. Do call me Harry. We're already

colleagues. I hope we're going to be friends." She turned and, taking Dee by one elbow, gestured toward her office with her other hand. "Come in, come in. Please make yourself comfortable." She took hold of the collar of Dee's parka. "Let me take your coat. Would you like some coffee?"

"Oh, that's okay," Dee said as she awkwardly flopped out of her parka. "I'm fine." She didn't care for coffee.

"Come on," Harry said familiarly. "It's no trouble. Join me. I'm addicted to the stuff."

"Okay," Dee said, laughing. "Coffee would be good, then."

Harry hung up Dee's jacket, said something to the secretary, and then closed her office door. The room surprised Dee. It was of painted cinder block, without a window, and very small, nothing like the elegant setting of Harry's films. It was also dimly lighted by only a desk lamp; the fluorescent ceiling lights were off. Behind Harry's desk was a swivel chair and to one side of it a small table holding a computer. On the other side of the room was a low bookcase filled mainly with manila folders. The only other furniture was an uncomfortable-looking plastic chair with chrome legs. Harry pointed cheerfully to it, and Dee sat down.

"Not exactly the Taj Mahal, I know," Harry said. "I have to go outside if I want to change my mind."

Dee smiled to acknowledge the joke.

"I want to thank you first of all for liking my program on Mrs. Soffel—which not everybody did, I'm afraid—and for saying so." Harry leaned forward, rested her forearms on either side of a manila folder lying on her desk blotter, and looked Dee full in the eyes. "I also want to say, Dee, how sorry I am not to have written you back. I meant to. I really did."

"Well," Dee said, "I was a little—"

But Harry cut her off. "No, Dee, I mean it—and I really need to hear myself apologize for things I don't want to repeat. It was unprofessional of me to do what I did, no matter how busy I was. I could at least have answered your questions."

"It's okay, Ms. Bromfield," Dee said self-consciously. "Really. It's okay."

"Harry, Dee, please." Harry smiled at her. "I told you, we're colleagues. And please understand that the main reason I'm sorry is that I really liked your letter. It's very perceptive. And I liked your term paper too. *Empty Calories for Inquiring Minds.* A cute title."

Dee squirmed internally. She wished Harry had used a word other than "cute."

"Here," Harry said, opening the manila folder in front of her. "Listen to this." She began to turn the pages of what Dee could see was her term paper. "Ah," she said putting a finger on a sentence with a green check mark alongside it. At that moment Judy came in with two white plastic cups of black coffee on a small tray. Harry took them both and gave one to Dee, who held it in both hands, pretending to sip.

"You don't use sugar or anything like that?" Harry asked. Dee shook her head.

"Now then," Harry said. "Listen to yourself."

> To speak of the "volcanic lusts" that drove Katherine Soffel to "violate her marriage vows" and "cavalierly abandon her children" is as libelous an oversimplification of her behavior as those tabloid headlines we all pretend not to be reading while waiting in line for the cashier at the supermarket: CIA CAPTURES UFO, THE PRESIDENT WAS HER LOVE SLAVE, MILK ROTS BONES. Is there nothing in what "drove" Katherine Soffel that involved courage or self-sacrifice or fidelity to anything?

Harry smiled and cocked her head. "Those are sentences with some sting to them, Dee. You really make your point."

There were sentences in her paper that Dee had worked harder on, but even so, she glowed with Harry's compliment. "Thank you," she said. "Thank you very much."

"I mean it, Dee. I don't wonder you won a prize. You deserved it."

Dee looked at Harry with some astonishment. She hadn't said anything in her letter about the prize.

Harry got to her feet. "In fact, the point you make

about the way the newspapers' sensationalism over-simplified what Kate did put me in mind of something."

She glided over to her bookcase with a spooky sort of grace, as though animated by something outside herself. The movement reminded Dee of an animal she'd seen once, but she couldn't remember the circumstances.

"Did you know," Harry said, bringing several manila folders back to her desk, "that at the same time Kate was visiting the Biddles, she said to her maid over and over that she was particularly interested in the sacrifice of Jesus?"

"No."

"Well, she did—but nobody then looked at any of the implications of the remark, you can bet."

Harry took the top manila folder, a great fat one, and pushed it across her desk to Dee. "It's all in here. Take a look at the testimony of the woman called Maggie Vogel. She was the Soffels' maid. The board of inquiry that looked into the escape interviewed her twice."

Dee opened the cover of the folder to a pile of pages typed in a very crude font. "TESTIMONY," the outside sheet read, and then under it:

Taken before the Prison Board of
Allegheny County Jail on Thursday, Friday,
and Saturday, January 30th, 31st, and

34

February 1st, 1902, in the matter of the
escape from said Jail of John and Edward
Biddle on Thursday, January 30th, 1902. Also
additional testimony taken on February 27,
1902.

The manuscript was at least two inches thick and was held together with two heavy rubber bands that ran crosswise to each other. Dee riffed the sheaf of pages at one corner. About three hundred altogether, she figured.

"This is . . . just what it says, the prison board's report? The whole thing?"

"It's a photocopy, yes."

"I thought those testimonies were secret."

Harry smiled. "They were." After a pause, she added, "Technically, they still are. Even so, that's the official transcript of all that was said—by the warden, the guards, everybody that was interviewed. Certain pieces of the testimonies were leaked to the press, but there aren't many people who've seen the whole thing, let alone who own a copy. That one's yours, by the way. I photocopied it myself."

"Thank you," Dee said. "Thank you very much."

"Consider it a belated answer to one of the questions in your letter."

"But where on earth—?"

"Did I get my copy?" Harry finished for her. "I'm

sorry, Dee, but I'm afraid I can't tell you that. I hope you understand."

"Oh, sure," Dee said. "Of course. I didn't mean—"

"I know you didn't." Harry smiled at her. "Don't worry about it. Let me show you some other things I have for you." She put another folder in front of Dee alongside the first, but kept her hand on top of it.

"Another thing you asked about in your letter was Kate's sworn confession. You said you didn't know she'd made one and asked where I'd found it. Now, did you check the newspapers for what they said about Kate *after* they described her being sentenced and packed off to prison? By 'after,' I mean a day later, or a couple of days later."

Dee just stared at Harry for a moment feeling stupid. She wouldn't have seen any point in checking the newspapers *after* Kate was sent to prison. "I don't think I did, no."

"Because you assumed—and it's a natural assumption—that once they'd bundled Kate off to jail, there was nothing left to report." Harry opened the cover of the second folder to a set of headlines beginning WOMAN'S STORY CLEARS MYSTERY IN BIDDLE CASE. "Now take a look at just the date on this first page."

In the upper right-hand corner of the page was a note: "Transcription from the *Pittsburgh Herald*, Sunday, May 11, 1902." Unlike the photocopied pages of the prison board's inquiry, this text was done on a word processor.

"Do you remember what day Kate was sentenced to prison?"

"No."

"Saturday, May tenth. She gave this interview a day later, right before she was taken out there. Always check the newspapers up to a week beyond their reporting of some key event in a sensational case, Dee. The Pittsburgh papers were all in tremendous competition with one another at the beginning of the century. Anything they could find—or invent—that suggested they had something the others didn't they'd bang into print as fast as they could, particularly in a Sunday edition, where they had a lot of pages to fill. *This* statement, as you can see, appeared in a Sunday edition and is almost certainly authentic."

"How do you know?"

Harry pointed to the bottom of the page:

Copyright, 1902
Reproduction of any portion of
this text is positively forbidden

"It's the only interview with Kate that was copyrighted. To copyright something was complicated in the early nineteen hundreds."

Dee smiled and nodded. "I see," she said. She was

getting an inside look at how a professional journalist worked.

"There are just two other things," Harry said, closing the folder Dee was looking at and putting it on top of the thick one. "Then we can get to what I know you've been wondering about: What's this lady after anyway?"

She held up a third folder, a slim one. "This is a checklist of pertinent facts about Kate: names, dates, that kind of thing. Not terribly exciting stuff, but useful to have gathered all in one place." She put the folder to the side, unopened. "And finally," Harry said, handing Dee a manila envelope, "this is the best answer I can give to the last questions in your letter: Where did I find the photograph of Kate that the newspapers retouched, and where did I find the one of her as a young woman? Again, I can't tell you where the photos came from, but you're welcome to copies of them—and I've put in some other photos you might not have seen. Of Peter, Kate's husband. Of the Biddles. Some of the guards."

Dee opened the folder and leafed through the pictures in it.

"Maybe Cory," Harry went on, "—that is his nickname, isn't it?—could paint some impressions from those pictures of Kate. He has a remarkable talent, one I'd like to help along, if I can. I saw that drawing of his in the newspaper, the one you posed for. *Girl in the Window*?"

Startled, Dee put the pictures facedown on the desk. Harry had found out about the prize for her senior paper. She also knew who her boyfriend was. What his nickname was. What he did. And she'd seen Cory's drawing of her. *Woman in the Window,* it was called.

Harry put her head back slightly and chuckled. "Relax, Dee. I haven't really invaded your life. That kind of information turns up about anyone you run a check on—which is station policy, by the way, not *my* idea.

"But," she went on, leaning forward, "I don't deny that I was, and am, interested in your life. And let me explain why." She reached across the desk and tapped one elegantly manicured nail on the backs of the pictures Dee had put down. "Suppose I told you that I have good reason to believe this lady kept a diary while she was in prison and maybe even after she was released too, a diary in which she tells what her connection with the Biddles and their escape really was. It's an even more sensational story than any that was imagined at the time, an almost unbelievable story, as a matter of fact. And suppose I told you that I think you and I, working together, have a chance of getting hold of this diary and seeing that Kate's story gets told to the world. Would you be interested?"

Dee moistened her lips. "Would I be interested? Are you kidding?"

Harry nodded and swiveled in her chair to face the side wall. She took off her glasses, then rubbed both eyes hard with the heels of her hands. When she turned back, her face seemed smaller, and she had that peculiar naked look some people who wear glasses have when they take them off.

"Now, I can't say for *sure* that the diary exists or that, even if it does, we can come up with it. And if we . . . decide to join forces, you're going to have a lot of . . . a lot of legwork to do, I'm afraid. There are things you'll have to do that I just can't. Are you still interested?"

"Of course."

"We'll get you a position as an intern at the station for the summer; they'll pay you something, not much, but something. I'd like us to get started before that, though, if that's okay."

"The sooner the better," Dee said, feeling her heart leap at the mention of an internship. It wasn't customary for businesses to offer them to freshmen.

"I'll give you a form to fill out before you leave, and you'll have to sign a few things—pledges not to steal soap out of the rest rooms here mostly. All right?"

"Sure."

For a few moments Harry stared down at her desk as though considering something. She nodded briefly. "Okay," she said, and then she said it again. "Okay."

She opened the top drawer of her desk and took out a half-empty pack of cigarettes and a small Bic lighter. She also took out a single piece of paper folded in half, which she lay in front of her. "Would you mind terribly if I had a cigarette, Dee? It helps me think."

"No, no," Dee said, waving one hand, though she hated the smell of cigarettes. "Please. Go right ahead."

Harry got up and slipped around her desk to stand almost alongside Dee under a ceiling vent. She moved like a jaguar, Dee suddenly realized. Harry reminded her of a jaguar she'd seen in the zoo once, levitating soundlessly from one level of its cage to another.

Harry lighted her cigarette, inhaled deeply, and blew a stream of smoke up at the vent. "There's a no smoking policy in the damned station," she said, looking ruefully at the burning end of the cigarette and then smiling down at Dee. "But I still can't kick the things completely." A faint but deep smell of musk came down to Dee along with the smell of burning tobacco. She wished Harry would go back behind her desk.

"Now, listen up," Harry said, shifting into the low voice of her broadcasts. "Last September, not long after the airing of my documentary, I got a telephone call from someone named Jury Hammond, who asked if he could come see me. He was a relative of Kate's, he said. His grandmother, who'd raised him, a woman

named Ellen Markwardt, was Kate's sister, and he said
he had some information from her that he believed
might answer some of what I'd called the unanswered
questions."

Harry winked at Dee conspiratorially. "Would
you guess that he had my full attention? I learned
later that he wasn't just making it up about his
grandmother. Actually, she was Kate's half sister.
Same father, different mothers. But she had indeed
raised Jury; he'd lived with her until she died, and
he still lives in the same place, an old house over in
Shadyside."

Harry stopped for a moment to take a flake of
tobacco from her tongue, and then she flicked the
ash from her cigarette toward the wastebasket in the
corner. "I also learned later that Jury's illegitimate.
That's how his grandmother came to raise him. She did
it alone too. His mother, Honor—if you can believe the
name—got herself knocked up at fifteen. No husband,
of course. She had the baby at home in that same
house in Shadyside and died not long after. I think it
was the shock of her death that killed Jury's grandfather less than six months later."

"My God!" Dee exclaimed.

Harry nodded. "Jury doesn't know I know any of
this, by the way. I don't know who his father was or
where his last name, Hammond, came from. I don't
think he knows either. It could be that the grand-

mother just made it up. Illegitimacy was a great disgrace in those days."

She paused as though thinking about what she'd just said. "Of course, it isn't the ideal character reference even today, is it?"

Dee smiled slightly without commenting.

"Anyway," Harry continued, "Jury claimed he'd never heard one word about Kate Soffel from his grandmother the whole time he was growing up. He knew who she was, of course, and the popular story about her, but he never knew he was related to her until just before his grandmother died. She was in the hospital when she told him everything—everything and then some, because according to Jury's grandmother, the *real* story about Kate and the Biddles had nothing to do with romantic love at all. Kate, with her husband's aid and endorsement, believed she was helping the Biddles escape purely to correct a miscarriage of justice."

"Ah," Dee couldn't keep herself from saying as she turned slightly and pointed up at Harry.

"Yes," Harry said, "I did touch on that as a possibility in my documentary. But I was only speculating, you see, wondering, and that was just one of several possibilities I was wondering about. Jury's grandmother wasn't speculating, though. Not according to him, at any rate. She was simply reporting what she'd read in Kate's diary. And there's more."

Harry paused and looked down at Dee and smiled.

"The more is that Kate was really being set up to be murdered. She, right along with the Biddles, had been set up by Kate's husband to be gunned down in the escape attempt, gunned down by him. Not one of the three of them was supposed to have gotten more than ten yards outside the prison door alive."

CHAPTER 5

D ee just stared up at Harry and then looked down, the skin on her back prickling. She shook her head slowly. "You said it was an unbelievable story. It is."

"It is until you think about it for a while. Think of what a hero good old Peter would have been, instantaneously too, for dropping the armed Biddles—one of him on two of them—and how much sympathy he'd have gotten for 'accidentally' killing his kidnapped wife in the course of doing his duty. In other words, if things had gone the way Peter planned, in about two minutes' time he'd have had a perfect way out of a marriage he'd grown tired of (not incidentally, he was his wife's only heir) and a perfect way of showing his relatives, all those politically connected uncles and nephews of his who were such big deals in the

Republican machine running the city, how wrong they'd been to see him as a klutz, to think that his nothing job as prison warden was the only thing he could handle. Why, the city might even have given him a medal or something, or at the very least, a pension in gratitude for his heroism, self-sacrifice, et cetera, et cetera. So off he'd go, his reputation made, all his wife's money and property tucked snugly in his pocket, and with all four of his children finally and fully his own, to be raised the way children *should* be raised."

"Is all that true, do you think?"

Harry took a long pull on her cigarette and blew two jets of smoke from her nose. She shrugged. "It could be. It fits all the facts—or rather, it can be made to fit all the facts. Whatever, it's one hell of a story, isn't it?"

"But how did Kate and the Biddles get away from the jail? Why weren't they all shot down just the way Kate's husband wanted?"

Harry shook her head. "I'm not sure. I think Jury knows, or knows what his grandmother told him Kate said anyway, but he was awfully vague about it with me."

"Maybe Peter lost his nerve at the last minute. Maybe he . . . had qualms of conscience or worried about his aim."

"I doubt it. I don't think Peter had much conscience. He was a real ice cube of a man, a planner, not somebody likely to change his plans at the last minute. You remember those five men who just showed up at Kate's divorce trial ready to swear they'd had sexual relations with her?"

"I thought they were never given a chance to testify."

"They weren't. That's my point. Peter had bribed them to be in court just in case he needed them."

"He *bribed* them?"

"Of course he bribed them. That's why not one of the five could be located after the trial to talk about his connection with Kate. Not one."

Dee didn't say anything. This was a brand-new Peter Soffel she was being introduced to—and, by implication, a brand-new Kate as well.

"And as for Peter worrying about his aim, that's not very likely either. He was a crack shot. He'd won prizes for pistol shooting." Harry laughed. "I think it was the only thing he was any good at—that and arranging murders."

Dee smiled thinly. "But what an ugly story it is," she said. "A man cold-bloodedly planning his wife's murder, her disgrace and murder, just for a little money."

Harry shrugged. "Not just for money, and maybe not so little. Perhaps it wasn't cold-blooded either. Kate must have been a bitch to live with, in and out of sanatoriums for depression all the time, getting into

47

one embarrassing popular cause after another. There could have been another woman too."

It was a lot for Dee to take in all at once. The new sequence of events flashed up in her mind as though on a computer screen. "Okay," she said, "so when things went wrong with Peter's plan and Kate was left alive, he kept her from talking by telling her that if she did, she'd never see her children again?"

Harry nodded. "So she never did, she never talked. Instead, she wrote out everything that happened in her diary—for her kids, you see, so they'd know in years to come that their mother was not the woman she'd been painted as being—and hid it under the floorboards of that little house she bought on Federal Street. In the hospital, though, dying of typhoid fever, she had second thoughts, and the diary she was planning to have her half sister Ellen deliver to her children she now made her promise to retrieve and destroy."

"I thought none of Kate's family came to see her in the hospital."

"So did I. That's what the newspapers said. But Jury told me Ellen sneaked in disguised as a nurse."

"Why did Kate want the diary destroyed, though?"

"I asked the same thing. Jury's answer was that Kate didn't want her kids to believe they carried the blood of a murderer in their veins." Harry paused a moment and then asked, "So what do you think Jury's grandmother did?"

Dee widened her eyes. "Well, I gather she didn't destroy the diary."

"She didn't. After reading it, she told Jury, she couldn't. So she hid it."

"Where?"

"Let me finish. When the grandmother was convinced that she too was dying, her conscience started to bother her. Part of her said that she should have burned the diary a long time before, just as she'd promised she would. But another part of her—she really hated Peter Soffel—wondered whether she should have made the diary public. If she'd done that, it would have cleared Kate's name, or so Jury's grandmother believed. On the other hand, Kate's name would have been cleared at the expense of Peter's, which, for the sake of her children, Kate had decided against. So Gram, as Jury calls her, ended up making *Jury* responsible for what to do. She made him promise *he'd* get the diary from where it was hidden, read it, and then make the decision of whether to burn or publish it. And the same day he promised her he would, she died."

Dee had trouble staying seated. "What'd he do?"

"For over twenty years he didn't do anything at all, and exactly why he waited so long was something else he was vague about. But last summer and fall he got serious about trying to locate the diary."

"Because of your film?"

49

"No. Even before that. I think because his retirement the spring before—he taught Latin at Thurston Academy for years—dumped a lot of time on his hands he didn't know what to do with. Also, I think maybe *his* conscience had started to bother *him*."

"So where'd the grandmother hide it?" Dee asked, trying to sound calmer than she felt.

Harry made a strange noise in her throat. "'Where'd the grandmother hide it?'" she repeated. "That's what we used to call the sixty-four-thousand-dollar question. All I know is that it's linked to the location of Kate's grave, which is supposedly somewhere in Smithfield Cemetery, but exactly where, no one's ever discovered. It was this grave Jury wanted me to help him find, because it's some kind of marker to where his grandmother hid the diary."

"What do you mean, 'marker'?"

"Oh, like the diary is buried six inches under a brass plaque three burial plots north and one plot west of where Kate lies. Something like that. He wouldn't tell me just *how* the grave's a marker, of course."

"Why wouldn't his grandmother have told him where the grave was?"

"She may have—and he may have forgotten after thirty years. Or maybe she just assumed he knew where it was already. Chances are, though, that she just wasn't very lucid about details right then. She was eighty-three, remember, and dying."

"So . . ." Dee gestured interrogatively. "Did you help him?"

Harry walked over to the corner and stubbed out her cigarette against the side of the wastebasket. She put the butt inside a piece of paper she balled up, dropped it in the wastebasket as well, and then went back to her desk.

"I tried, Dee," Harry said once she was seated again. "I really did try. And not just because he promised me we'd share what was in the diary if I became his partner."

Dee waited, thinking Harry would explain, but the journalist only stared down at her desk with narrowed eyes. After a time, Dee said, "I gather you and Jury aren't working together . . . now?"

Harry laughed. Not a nice laugh. "We never did work *together*, really. But I was careful never to say so or to tell him I thought he was trying to get over on me either, even though I'm sure now that that's what he was trying to do. I don't think he ever had any intention of sharing the diary with me. He was always swimmy in dealing with my questions about what he knew, like how he'd found out Kate had a large insurance policy on her life." She laughed the same unpleasant laugh again. "I've seen the evasion technique before, God knows—particularly from men.

"But I never ducked any of the questions he asked

me about Kate. I shared my materials with him, just the way I am with you. I told him all I knew, everything I knew. And though, as I'm sure you know, no direct descendant of Kate's has ever come forward, I even tried through the Internet, which is real rocket science to a mossback like Jury, to find him one of Kate's indirect descendants. His thought was that maybe another distant relation of hers like him would know where she was buried. But we didn't turn up anyone or anything. Then—" Harry stopped without finishing.

"Then what?"

Harry rolled her eyes. "This is a little embarrassing. He hit on me, is what. Or tried to. Can you imagine? An old goat like that?"

"Were you . . . okay?"

"Oh, sure," Harry said easily. "I should have seen it coming, I suppose. He was always looking me over when he thought I wasn't watching. It came as a surprise, though. One night late last fall he called me at home. He said that he was sorry he hadn't seemed to trust me and asked if I'd give him another chance. And then he invited himself over."

She grinned and tossed her hair into sparkly waves. "He came up behind me when I was making a drink and grabbed me." She clapped her hands on to her breasts. "Just like that. It surprised me more than anything else."

Dee could feel herself color. "Jeez," she said, feeling like a jerk the moment she had.

"The real problem was the fallout between us afterward. *He* was the one who couldn't accept what he'd done. He wouldn't answer any of my phone calls. I haven't seen or heard from him since that night."

She paused, but Dee, who was getting a little uncomfortable with her gee-whizzing straight-man role, decided not to ask the obvious questions.

Harry smiled, put her glasses on, and opened the folded paper she'd put on her desk earlier. After scanning it, she passed it to Dee. "Tell me what you make of this."

It was a newspaper want ad blown up to about three times its original size:

> Now is the time for all good men and women
> wishing to aid in the vindication of
> Katherine Dietrich Miller
> to come forward and enlist their services.
> 555-1278

"This is his telephone number?"

"Oh, yes. The ad's been run for two Sundays now in the personal column of the *Tribune-Review*."

Dee read it again. "And he uses the name Miller for Kate because only somebody who'd studied the case would know that that was the name she took after she got out of prison."

"Smart girl," Harry said, raising a hand in acknowledgment. "Smart girl. He wants somebody who knows about Kate and is . . . reasonably sympathetic to her. That means he still hasn't got hold of the diary.

"Now, partner, tell me how you factor in one last piece of information. Not long after Jury and I had our little love affair, he had a heart bypass operation in Shadyside Hospital and damn near died."

Dee just stared at Harry's ironical half smile, but not in bewilderment. She had a feeling she knew where Harry was going.

"Well," Harry said, tossing her hair again and leaning back in her swivel chair. Her jutting breasts made Dee think of Jury's hands on them, and she looked down at her lap. "Let me tell you how *I* factor it in." She laced her fingers together and clasped them behind her head. "Jury's desperate, as I read it. He hears the meter running on his life and wants someone to go to work for him on Kate's case."

Then Harry sat forward, put her forearms on her desk, and leaned over them toward Dee. "I think he's looking for someone like you, Dee. For someone exactly like you."

Was it just Dee's imagination or was Harry overdoing it a little? "Okay," she said. "So you want me to call him."

"Of course. Call him. Follow his directions. And stay in touch with me. That's all you have to do. He's got a plan of some sort, or he wouldn't be advertising the way he is. So the first thing we do is discover what the plan is. Then we'll work out how to play it, okay?"

Whatever else she knew, Dee knew also it was the chance of a lifetime she was being offered and she was nodding her head even before she spoke. "Okay," she said. "Absolutely. Do you really think that the diary will say . . . what the grandmother, Gram, says it does?"

"Dee," Harry said, with perhaps a trace of impatience in her voice, "start thinking like a journalist here. It doesn't matter what the diary says, or even whether what it says is true. What matters is that Kate said something about what happened with the Biddles that no one knows she said. That's a story—one that could be worth a lot to both of us, do you see? In fact, there may be even more of a story we can get out of that diary than anybody's yet imagined. Did you know, for instance, that the symptoms of typhoid fever, and that's what killed Kate, are very similar to the symptoms of arsenic poisoning—and that in 1909 you could buy arsenic at a corner drugstore?"

Again, Dee just stared. Kate might have been *murdered*?

Harry snorted a laugh at her expression.

"Dee," she said, "all I'm trying to do is give you

some sense of just how many stories may be possible with this diary. It's a gold mine. But you never know how much gold's in a mine or what the quality of it is until you tunnel down and get it, yes?"

"Yes," Dee said quickly. "Of course. I'm with you." She was not going to sound—or look—like some naive kid to Harry again. "Let's run through how you think I ought to answer Jury's ad, and I can call him tonight."

CHAPTER 6

It was late Sunday afternoon, a gray and grizzled February day. Dee and Cory were sitting cross-legged on the living room floor facing the couch where Megan lay cocooned in a blanket, her feet engulfed by a pair of enormous slippers in the shape of mallard ducks. They'd been a Christmas present from Dee in wry acknowledgment of her roommate's constant complaints about how cold their apartment was. To one side of Dee, in a pile, were all the materials Harry had given her.

The three friends were just finishing the second of two large pizzas with everything. Dee's treat. "Payola," Megan had called it and with some justification. Ever since meeting with Harry, Dee had not been able to focus on much other than her upcoming meeting with Jury Hammond and how it might connect with the discovery of a new Kate Soffel. Dee knew this obsession had begun to get on her room-mate's nerves.

Megan dropped a piece of pizza crust on her plate and pointed at the pile of manila folders.

"Now, would I be *dead* wrong in imagining you're going to ask us to sing for our supper? Maybe you've got a recipe for Mace you'd like us to help you test out before you go to meet your dirty old man."

"No," Cory said, grinning. "I'm going to be the Mace."

The plan was to have Cory sit in a booth across the room while Dee met with Jury at the Dancing Goats Coffee Shop in Shadyside tomorrow night.

"Weeelll," Dee said, opening the topmost manila folder on the pile to her left and taking out some stapled packets, "there is one thing I'd like you to glance at. I'm planning to give this to Jury should the occasion arise, and I wondered . . ." She handed a packet to Cory and one to Megan without finishing her sentence. But then she added, "This won't take long, I promise."

"You really push the envelope sometimes, you know," Megan said, a bit testily Dee thought.

Throwing off the blanket, Megan sat up and banged both duck feet on top of the coffee table. The con-trast of her short vigorous body and jet black hair and eyes with Dee's willowy height and pale coloring had always seemed to people who knew them a good guide to their temperamental differences. But the two had been friends since fifth grade, and Dee often thought of Megan as her sister. Indeed, after Dee's parents had divorced and moved away from Pittsburgh, she'd lived with Megan's family part of last summer until the two of them moved to an apartment to be near Pitt's campus. The first packet was titled:

The *Pittsburgh Herald* Confession of Katherine Soffel (May 11, 1902): Some Unanswered Questions

and there were fifteen numbered points underneath it.

"Hey, Dee, come on!" Megan yelped upon seeing the small, single-spaced type. "Tomorrow's a school day, you know."

"You don't have to read it *all*. Just tell me what you think of the first three or four points I make, how I come across."

In reading through Harry's photocopy of Kate's confession to the newspaper, Dee had noticed a number of comments she wouldn't have expected Kate to make. Was it possible that she was attempting to tip readers off that the generally accepted story of the Biddles' escape was not the real story at all? Harry said she too had wondered about this and encouraged Dee to write down what she'd seen. The first four items of Dee's list read:

1. Both Biddles, Kate says, had had "poison and knives hidden in their cells" for months. Yet she also says their cells were "carefully searched" daily without this ever being discovered—or without their guns and saws being found either. Is she implying that these things were all deliberately overlooked?

2. When Kate says that "the testimony given before the prison board was not correct," is she referring only to the guards' testimony? Or does she mean to imply that people like her husband and her maid, Maggie Vogel, had not told the truth either?

3. "When the boys did leave the jail," Kate says, "they were not prepared. They were forced to go." But why were the Biddles *not* prepared after having cut through the bars of their cells almost two weeks earlier? And who or what "forced" them to go?

4. "I refused . . . to buy the saws," Kate says, but she also says, "saws were secured for the boys." Where, then, did the saws (let alone the Biddles' guns) come from—since Kate was never identified as having purchased them? Somebody else *had* to have been involved in the escape.

Both Megan and Cory read silently for so long that it made Dee anxious. "What's wrong?" she asked, looking at Megan.

It was Cory who responded. "Nothing. I think you sound like you know what you're talking about. That's what you want, isn't it?"

"Of course it's what she wants," Megan snapped before Dee could say anything. "Isn't that what the Spider Lady told you to sound like? You better change your title, though, if you expect Jury to believe you don't know Harry. It's the title of her film."

"Of course," Dee said, crossing out "Some Unanswered Questions" on her copy. "Thank you." Megan's irritability made her uneasy.

Cory pulled up his legs to prop one of the empty pizza cartons against his thighs so he could doodle on the back. Dee had never known him to be without a small case of felt-tipped pens. He drew whenever he had the chance on whatever happened to be around—napkins, envelopes, bills and receipts, even newspapers. He drew particularly in the face of tension; Cory didn't like confrontations.

"It's amazing nobody ever saw any of this before," he said with his head down.

"Nobody except the Spider Lady," Megan said. "*She* saw all this *first*—which is why she likes Dee's idea so much."

"Hey, Megan!" Dee cried. "Cut it out. What's with you anyway?"

"Ladies, ladies," Cory said, putting a hand on Dee's shoulder. "Let's remember we're friends—and that

61

we've all just had a great free meal. All except Dee, I mean."

Megan kept her head down and flipped the pages of the packet Dee had given her. "What's this?" she asked rudely, holding up the last couple of typed sheets.

Katherine Dietrich Soffel Miller
Data

I. Key Dates

• Kate born: July 26, 1867.

Kate was 19, Peter 22.

• Kate married: December 9, 1886.

• Kate's children born: Irene (1887); Margarite (1888); Edwin (1891); Clarence (1894).

ages at escape
14, 13, 10, 7

Kate was 35. Ed was 24.

• Biddles escape from Allegheny County Jail: 3:10 A.M., Thursday, January 30, 1902.

• Biddles and Kate apprehended outside Butler: 5 P.M., Friday, January 31, 1902.

• Kate pleads "nolo contendere" before court. No trial: May 5, 1902.

• Kate sentenced to prison for two years: May 10, 1902.

• Kate's interview with *Pittsburgh Herald*: May 11, 1902.

Found guilty of adul. pros. E.d. claimed guilty with 5 other men (on evid. of Maggie Vogel) but evid. not Taken in court.

• Kate divorced by Peter Soffel on grounds of adultery. Trial: October 21-22, 1903.
Kate not present at trial. Divorce granted December 16, 1903.

• Kate released from prison: December 10, 1903 (five months off for good behavior).

• Kate enters West Penn Hospital: August 22, 1909.

• Kate dies West Penn Hospital: August 30, 1909 (of typhoid fever).

on Sept. 1? 2? 3? where in cem.? Under what name? Church records? (No!)

• Kate is buried in Smithfield Cemetery, Pittsburgh.

II. Miscellaneous Information

Kate was 14 at death.

1. Mother of Kate was Maria Louisa, born in Germany, 1844-1881.

2. Father of Kate was Conrad H. Dietrich, born in Germany (1840?). After death of Maria (Kate's

mother) he remarried (a year later) Katherine Charlotte Wild (widow) on April 25, 1882.

3. Peter (Kate's husband) remarries in 1907 (Margaret Taggert—a widow?). He dies September 11, 1936. *children?*

4. Kate (and mother) were members of Smithfield Evangelical Church.

5. Kate at Western Pennsylvania Penitentiary was prisoner 3509 on A range. *pos. Haller?*

6. Kate had younger brother, Julius (?), sister married to Jacob Miller, and sister Ellen.

Ellen was ½ sister, Born 1889 (of Kate's father and Charlotte Wild). Ellen m. Henry Markwardt. daughter Honon (b. 1907). Honon has son Jurr Hammond, 1922. (She is unmarried and 15) Honon dies in childbirth. Henry dies 6 mos. later. Ellen raises Jurr and dies in 1990 at 88.

7. Addresses:

Kate's father: 22 Southern Avenue, Mt. Washington.

Peter: 73 Maple Terrace, Mt. Washington.

Haller?
Kate's sister (Mrs. Jacob Miller): 26 Southern Avenue, Mt. Washington.

Kate: 903 Federal Street, Pittsburgh, North Side (took name of Miller) (Bell phone: Cedar 731R).

Jurr Hammond, 350 Spahn St. PT569. 15232

8. Dorman (turned state's evidence against Biddles) paroled November 1, 1923.

9. Judge McClung (who granted divorce to Peter Soffel) also sentenced the would-be assassin of H. Clay Frick (Alexander Berkman) to Western Pennsylvania Penitentiary. Willa Cather roomed at the judge's house for several years and was the friend of his daughter, Isabelle.

10. The crime for which Biddles were convicted was the murder of grocer Kahney during a night burglary on April 11, 1901. The Biddles were captured (on information by Dorman) April 12. In the taking of the Biddles, Officer Patrick Fitzgerald was killed (by bullet from a fellow officer? Robert Gray?) and Biddles were blamed.

11. Kate's daughter Irene married someone named Pedigo? 1910?

12. Play about Mrs. Soffel and Biddles registered December 17, 1903. *A Dangerous Woman: A Melodrama in Three Acts.*

(No copies exist?)

13. Undertaker handling Kate was Lutz and Beinhauer.

— all records of firm before 1952 were destroyed by fire.

14. Kate had a niece, Sara Soffel, who was about fifteen when the Biddles escaped. Sara was first female Supreme Court judge in state of Pennsylvania.

"It's data on the life of Katherine Dietrich Soffel Miller," Dee said huffily in response to Megan's question. "What's it look like?"

Cory stopped drawing and turned in his packet to the pages Megan was questioning.

For a while no one said anything.

"Come on, honey," Cory said. "It's a fair question. Are these pages for Jury too?"

Dee took a deep breath, puffed her cheeks, and then blew the air out. "They're just some things I want to keep straight for myself. Dates and stuff." And then she glanced pointedly at Megan and added, "Not all of us have garbage can memories, you know."

Megan could hear a phone number once and remember it forever.

"And whose handwriting is this in the margins?" Megan asked, turning the pages of the data section. "It's not yours."

"No. It's Harry's. The data things are too."

Then Megan raised her head and looked at Dee. "Now, let me see if I have this right," she said, her voice full and throaty. Megan was studying to be a lawyer like her father; every time she used what Dee called her "lawyer's voice," they ended up having a fight.

"These things that you just want to keep straight for yourself, these things that Harry put together and wrote notes on, you're going to use with Jury and tell him *you* wrote, so he'll see how smart you are. Have I got the picture?"

Dee felt her cheeks flame.

"If you're implying I'll be lying to Jury and are trying to make me feel guilty about it, forget it. I don't. Not one bit. Not after what he did to Harry. I mean, he treated her like a *whore.*" Dee held out one hand, palm up. "Look, Megs, I'm not even working with Jury yet. I'm only a candidate. What's wrong with trying to make myself look like the strongest candidate I can? Harry thinks it's a good idea."

"Oh, Harry, Harry, Harry," Megan said in disgust. And then she sneered. "'The strongest *candidate'?!* Give me a break here, Dee! How many people do you think have called about the ad—and how many of them have written prize-winning papers on Kate Soffel? You're a shoo-in for the job and you know it!"

Dee looked up, just about ready to blast her roommate for her tone, but then thought better of it. Megan had a point, after all. Dee dropped her head into one hand, rubbed her forehead, and laughed a brief, nervous laugh. "I guess it does bother me some to . . . to play a role this way. I even said so to Harry."

"And what'd she say?" Megan asked.

"She said all investigative reporters have to withhold certain things from the people they talk to. If they didn't, there wouldn't be any investigative reporting."

"Clever," Megan said. "That's really clever."

Out of the corner of her eye Dee could see that Cory's doodle was turning Megan's duck slippers into a pair of arrowheaded dragons. She studied her roommate for a time and then said, "Well, it's plain what you think of Harry anyway."

"Dee," Megan said, "it isn't just that I don't like her. There's something funny going on here, can't you see that? There's something almost creepy in the way she's suddenly glommed on to you. She's holding back something."

"*What's* funny? *What's* she holding back?"

Megan scratched the back of her neck hard, a gesture of irascibility with her. "All right," she said. "Let's fast-forward a bit here. Let's say you get the job with Jury, which you will, and go to work for him and find the diary. What do you do then? Grab it away from him and run to Harry?"

Dee stared at her. "Do you really think I'd do that?"

"It's a question of what Harry will expect of you, Dee. Let's take a different scenario. Suppose you find the diary and *Jury* wants to run away with it, keep it just for himself. Or suppose he decides to burn it, the way Kate wanted, but without even letting you read it first or without letting Harry read it at all. Will you just stand there and watch him go off into the sunset or watch the diary go up in smoke? You think Harry will let that happen?"

Dee considered it. "It doesn't make any sense that Jury would go to all this trouble to locate the diary just so he could burn it."

"It could make sense," Cory put in, "if he's a certain kind of guy. I think Harry's right that Jury thinks time is running out for him. When my grandfather, my father's father, was diagnosed with cancer and given six months to live, he gathered up all the letters and photographs he'd saved and burned them in the fireplace. When my father asked him why, he said that everything he'd burned was his to do with as he liked. He said he had a right to put his life in order."

Dee looked over at him. "That's a terrible story," she said. "I can't even imagine a man like that."

"The thing is," Cory said, his eyes on his drawing, "we really don't know what kind of a guy this Jury is, do we? No matter what Harry said."

"Not any more than we know who Harry is," Megan added.

Dee chewed on the side of her lower lip, thinking.

"Okay, what about this? Jury can't just walk away with the diary, or burn it, because Harry's got a contract with him—the same way she does with me."

Megan shook her head and smiled. "I asked Dad about contracts like that when I talked to him on the phone this morning. Hypothetically, of course," she added quickly upon seeing Dee's expression, "just hypothetically. Dad said that if the contract is like the one you signed, it has no binding force on Jury at all; it's simply a standard way the TV station has of protecting its property, intellectual and otherwise. But the diary doesn't belong to the station. It belongs to Kate's heirs. And Jury—you were the one who told us this—is the only one of Kate's heirs currently available."

Dee was beginning to feel panicked. "But you don't know what kind of a contract Harry signed with Jury—or, for that matter, with me either."

"I only know what you told me you signed, and we don't know whether Jury signed a contract with Harry at all."

"Meaning that Harry lied to me. But why would she lie about something like that? If there is no contract and the diary belongs just to Jury, what good would getting it be to Harry?"

"What *good* would it be to her? Are you kidding? Think of the money somebody like Harry could make if she had sole rights to something like Kate's diary. And all she'd have to do to get them would be to grab the diary, put it in a safe place until Jury dies—not exactly an eternity, to judge from his health history— and then make up any story she likes about how she got it. Who else, besides us, even knows that there *is* a diary? And who would believe us over the Spider Woman?"

Cory put down his pen, and he and Dee looked

first at each other and then at Megan. After a time, Dee sighed. "Boy," she said, shaking her head, "you really don't like her, do you?"

"No, I don't. I hate the way she oozes all that drop-dead sex, and I hate the way she manipulates. Last fall she couldn't even call or write you a thank-you note for your letter. Now, when she needs you, she throws you a parade of roses. I don't trust her."

Megan then hunched forward, resting her fore-arms on her knees. After a time, she smiled bitterly and said, "And I guess I better admit that I . . . I hate the way you make a kind of god out of her."

So that was it. Megan was jealous. Dee went over to the couch, sat down next to Megan, and put her arm around her shoulders. "You're my best friend, Megs," she said, "and I know you're worried about me, but could we just give Harry the benefit of the doubt here—for a while anyway? I understand she's using me; she as much as said so herself. But it's an awfully big thing she's cutting me in on too. She didn't have to say she'd get me an internship, you know. She didn't have to say she'd help Cory. She's been nothing but friendly and decent. She even said she wanted to take the three of us to dinner. Could we just try to imagine that it might be a straight deal she's offering me? I know I must have sounded like I think Harry walks on water the last few days, but I don't really. I'm going to take things slow, I promise you, which is why I made sure she knew—and I'll make sure Jury knows—that you guys are going to be working with me every step of the way."

Dee paused and then said, "This is the biggest chance I'll ever have to get something I really want just for myself—the way you want the law, the way Cory has his art."

CHAPTER 7

In addition to Cory, whom she pretended not to know, there were only six or seven other people in the Dancing Goats Coffee Shop when Dee entered. Her first impression of the older man who rose to his feet from a booth was that of an ancient bird of prey. He had a thin jutting nose, close-set inquiring eyes, and he held his head forward slightly, as though homing in on something. Up close, however, there was a sad gray cast to his expression. It was hard to imagine that this was the guy who'd grabbed Harry. He looked about as predatory as a dead plant.

"Mister . . . Hammond?" Dee asked tentatively, extending her hand.

"In the flesh," he said in a peculiar, rasping voice. He leaned forward slightly and then back again—a bow, Dee realized. Then he took her extended hand not in a handshake, but as though picking up an object. With his other hand he gestured at the seat opposite his. He had not taken his coat off, Dee noticed as she deposited her backpack on the booth seat and shrugged herself out of her parka. Jury's coat was real sheepskin; she could see its fleece lining where he'd opened it down the front. On the table in front of him was a napkin, a glass of water, and a tiny cup of liquid, black as tar.

"Cold out," Dee said with a smile, rubbing her hands together. She turned in her seat to look toward the front of the coffee shop, where bursts of snow were breaking silently on the high glass windows like handfuls of confetti. It had been snowing the same way all day: furiously for a bit, then stopping, and then starting again.

From behind a long stainless-steel and glass counter filled with a lot of exotic-looking pastries, a waitress appeared with a napkin and glass of water for Dee. "Maybe I'll order something later," Dee said.

Jury waited until they were alone.

"You're ten minutes late, Ms. Armstrong," he said in his strange, whispering voice. "I don't like that." He said it without smiling. The strangeness of Jury's voice was oddly familiar.

Actually, she hadn't been late—she was rarely late for anything—Cory had been. She'd wanted him already settled in the coffee shop before she entered. Dee was on the verge of making an excuse, but she decided against it. "I don't like it either," she said. "I'm sorry." And then she added, "It's Dee, by the way. Dee Armstrong."

Jury studied her for a moment, though what his expression meant she couldn't tell, and then he nodded curtly and reached down below the table. She heard the snick of a briefcase latch, and the term paper she'd sent him was on the table between them.

He put on a pair of glasses, moved his espresso or whatever it was to one side, and began turning pages, just as Harry had. The margins of his copy, though, were covered with notes.

"How'd you get interested in Katherine Soffel?" he asked without looking at her. The question was one Harry had told Dee to try to answer as simply as possible.

"We saw the movie in my Pittsburgh history course, and I got interested in how much of it was true. Actors like Mel Gibson and Diane Keaton can make you forget what the facts are."

"I see. Do you still find her interesting, even though, as you say in your paper, we may never know the truth about her motives?"

His voice was the sort that made Dee want to clear her own throat, and she suddenly realized where she'd heard one like it before. When she was growing up, a police detective whose nickname was Licorice had lived next door. He spoke just as Jury did, the result of a smashed larynx, her father had told her.

"Oh, yes. I think she's fascinating. It may have been a crazy thing she did leaving her children that way, but you have to admit that she really put herself on the line for what she believed in. She had . . . courage, the kind of courage I think women today ought to respect."

"Why women today?"

Dee frowned, thinking. "Well, what she had to stand up to was a very today kind of problem, don't you think? The massive media assaults, the incredible rushes to judgment—"

"Yes, yes, yes," he said impatiently. "Those are certainly phrases we hear all the time. But do you mean it's women rather than men who ought to respect Kate, or do you mean it's women particularly?"

Dee wasn't sure she knew what he was after. "I mean women particularly."

He didn't look up from her paper. "Continue, please," he said after a time.

And that was the way their conversation proceeded. He'd ask her a question and she'd answer it, and then, after a pause, he'd ask her a question about her answer, and then after another pause, he'd ask still another question—all the while turning the pages of her paper without looking at her at all. She was glad she'd never been one of his students.

Finally, Dee broke one of his long pauses with a question of her own. "Are you going to tell me what you think?" she asked, pointing at her marked-up paper. "It looks like you've had a lot of . . . disagreement with what I wrote."

He smiled, a cold thin smile. "I assumed, I hope correctly, that this copy of your paper was mine to keep?"

"Of course."

"I was a teacher for many years. Latin. At Thurston Academy. Annotating texts, I'm afraid, is rather a habit of mine."

Dee nodded and waited. Something told her not to try to engage Jury Hammond in small talk.

After a time, he smiled again. He probably allowed himself three a day, Dee thought.

And then he did look up from her paper directly into her eyes. It was a shock to Dee. His irises were of such pale gray, they seemed almost white.

"I can see why you won your prize," he said. "It is not a stupid paper. You write clearly at least, and you cover the material that you found to cover competently. If you were a student of mine, I would mark you as someone with definite potential."

So he too had found out about her prize. It had been Harry's idea that Dee not mention it either over the phone or when she mailed him her paper. "It'll mean more if he finds out about it himself, just the way I did."

"May I ask, however," Jury went on, "speaking of what you found to cover, why there is no reference in your bibliography to Kate's statement in the *Pittsburgh Herald*? Do you know that statement?"

Dee breathed a silent thank-you to the universe as she took the list of questions she'd written about the statement from her backpack.

"I know the statement *now*," Dee said, "but I didn't last year. My research was pretty . . . skimpy first time through." She shook her head. "I'm still not sure what Kate was doing in the statement, though," she said, handing her list of questions to Jury. She'd retitled it "The *Pittsburgh Herald* Confession of Katherine Soffel: Smoky Signals?"

He read intently, or so it seemed to her, turning back to reread certain passages several times. When he finished, he took off his glasses, put them on the table, and stared at her. With more respect? More suspicion?

"You made these questions up all by yourself? You didn't have the help of a . . . a teacher, someone like that?"

"No. They're mine." She was very, very glad she'd listened to Megan about the risk of using Harry's data sheet.

Jury nodded and continued looking at her. "Remarkable," he said, putting his glasses on again and going back to what she'd written. "You've noticed some things . . . ," he trailed off, reading. "Your number fifteen, for instance, where you say that Kate described the fugitives' path from the prison to Union Station so as to make it clear they were moving in a circle in

78

order to avoid something ahead of them rather than escape something behind. That's a fascinating insight. How did you determine it was a circle they were moving in, however? Some of the streets she mentions, like Tunnel, for instance, are gone now."

He was testing her, Dee knew, something for which Harry had warned her to be ready. So she explained how she'd discovered the circularity of the fugitives' escape route by tracing it on a 1905 Pittsburgh city map in the library.

Harry had also warned her to watch out for slips, like the temptation to mention Kate's *half* sister, who had never been referred to that way in the press. "In fact, it won't do any harm to play dumb about a few details so Jury can show off how much he knows," Harry had suggested. "He's no different that way from any other man."

"Kate's children," Jury said abruptly. "Do you remember who they were?"

"Their names, you mean?"

He nodded briefly.

Dee did know their names, but she screwed her face up as though trying to recall them.

"Let's see. She had four children, two boys and two girls. Maggie was the oldest, I think. Then Irene, then Clarence, and . . . Edward?"

"Actually, Irene was the eldest and Maggie next, a year younger. And it was Ed*win* not Ed*ward.* He was the third child, by the way. Clarence was the baby. He was only eight at the time of the Biddles' escape. How about Kate's lawyers? Do you remember who they were?"

God! Dee thought. She hadn't a clue as to the names of Kate's lawyers. But she also had a feeling that it didn't matter. She knew she'd really stopped him with her list and her research to discover the fugitives' escape route. She would have bet that Jury was only trying to regain the advantage in their conversation.

"Let's see now," Dee said, crossing her arms on the table and staring down at them. "Her doctor was a man named Briggs, I remember that, and the judge who sentenced her to prison was . . . Fraser, I think. But her lawyers . . ." She didn't finish.

"Do you happen to remember the name of the judge who gave Kate's husband his divorce?"

She did, but she shook her head and smiled in a way she hoped suggested poise—and patience. "I'm afraid not."

"McClung," Jury said offhandedly. "Judge S. A. McClung. He was the same judge who sentenced the would-be assassin of Henry Clay Frick to Western Penitentiary. Alexander Berkman? The anarchist? Did you know that he and Kate were both in Western Penitentiary at the same time?"

"Why, no," Dee murmured, leaning back in the booth, letting him run with things.

"And Willa Cather, the novelist?" Jury had raised his voice a bit; there was a kind of barkiness to his pronouncements. "She lived in McClung's house, roomed there. She was a friend of McClung's daughter, Isabelle."

Dee put her forearms on the table and leaned over them. "May I ask you something now, Mr. Hammond?"

"I'm sorry," he said. "I'm chattering." He gestured invitationally with one hand. "Please."

"Would you mind telling me why *you're* so interested in Katherine Soffel? Are you doing a book or what?"

Jury stared at her for a moment and then looked off. After a time, he nodded. "Fair question," he said. "It's a fair question. However, I'd like to ask you one other thing first—well, two other things—before I address it, if you don't mind."

He then leaned over the table, just as she had. Their faces were rather uncomfortably close for Dee, and she suddenly flashed on an image of him with Harry, but she resisted the impulse to pull back. Jury tapped the copy of her paper that lay between them with his forefinger. "You say toward the end of your paper that in addition to not having the full story of Kate's motivation, we may not have the full story about what happened with Kate and the Biddles either. You suggest that she may have been victimized even beyond the way her newspaper critics and Arthur Forrest in that scandalous book of his criticized her. But you do not say what form you believe this victimization may have taken or who you believe might have been responsible for it. Correct?"

Dee's mouth was dry. It was a good paraphrase of the end of her paper, but those same pages, at Harry's suggestion, were a revision of what she'd written originally. Had Jury somehow discovered the change?

"Right," Dee nodded in response to Jury's question. "That's correct."

"If you had to guess, though—," Jury began, but then he stopped himself, raised one hand with the index finger pointed at the ceiling, and in a moment started again. "Let me put it this way. Let's suppose you had evidence, irrefutable evidence, that someone, a single person, had indeed been out to victimize Kate with the Biddles' escape, had planned, in fact, to kill her or to have her killed, right in the middle of it and right along with the two condemned men. And let's further suppose that from the"—he fished in the air with his raised hand—"the dramatis personae of the case, you had to come up with the name of the person who engineered things. Who would you think it to be? And please do not bother saying that you do not know for certain. I am asking you to make an intelligent guess."

Jury never took his gray-white eyes off hers. His conditions and questions were dizzying, like a mirror maze.

"You mean, if Kate was being set up, who do I think set her up?"

"Yes."

"Her husband," Dee said without hesitation.

For a moment Jury stared at her, licking his lower lip. An expression came over his face as though of triumph. Then he straightened up in his seat, nodding. "Peter the weasel," he rasped bitterly. "Of course. Peter the rat. You ask why I am doing what I am doing? My research is to find what will expose that monster for what he really was."

Aha! Dee thought. Of course he had no plans to burn the diary.

Jury was looking at Dee, but all of a sudden he seemed not to be seeing her any longer, and a quick grimace twisted his features. "Excuse me for a moment," he said, digging into his coat pocket. He put something under his tongue and leaned all the way back in the booth, eyes closed. His face was ashen. It looked two-dimensional, like something drawn on paper. He was sweating.

Dee was immobilized at first and then got to her feet. "Are you okay?" she asked anxiously. "Can I get you anything? Some water?" Out of the corner of her eye she saw that Cory had gotten up as well.

"Nothing, thank you," Jury whispered without opening his eyes. "I have what I need." For a while he breathed very deeply and then more regularly. Gradually his face began to regain its contours. He opened his eyes and looked up at Dee. "Only a temporary indisposition, I assure you, my dear." He took a sip of water.

Dee sat back down and waited, turning her own water glass around and around on the table. She saw that Cory had sat down again too. After a time, Jury straightened up and mopped his face with his handkerchief. He then gathered his sheepskin coat closely around him and drank about half his water. When he spoke, his voice was less raspy, more like a purr.

"Now, I want you to listen to me very carefully. My interest in Kate Soffel is not scholarly. That is, I have more than just a scholar's interest in her. Kate was a relative of mine." And then, somewhat haltingly, Jury went on to tell Dee the same story about Kate and his grandmother and the hidden diary that Harry had said he'd told her. "So you see," he concluded by saying, "what I need is a research assistant to help me locate the diary that I believe will prove Kate's innocence. You, Dee, are precisely the sort of person I was advertising for, that I was hoping for. In fact, you seem almost too good to be true."

CHAPTER 8

"May I ask you," Jury went on, "how it was you came upon my ad in the personal column? You do not make a habit, do you, of reading that section of the newspaper?"

Instantly, Dee was alert again. "He's going to find some way of asking you whether we know each other," Harry had coached her. "He may do it directly, or he may slither into the question through some kind of back door, but he's going to ask. So plan now how you're going to field it. And please bear in mind, Dee, that the bottom line here is, if Jury learns we spoke—no more than that—he'll have nothing further to do with you."

"Oh, heavens no," Dee laughed in response to Jury's question. "I don't read the personals at all, really. My roommate, Megan, does, though. She's been my best friend for a long time, and she listened to me about

Kate the whole time I was working on my term paper. Every Sunday she reads the newspaper from cover to cover, from start to finish, I mean."

All of which was perfectly true.

"So Megan found the ad?"

"Well," Dee replied, laughing again, "I certainly didn't find it myself."

That too was the truth.

Then Jury did put the question directly. "Do you know Harriet Bromfield, by any chance?"

Dee was prepared. She dropped her head and stared down at the table. "In a way," she said. Then after a moment, she looked up. "You saw that program she did last fall, I imagine? On the unanswered questions in the Kate Soffel case?"

Jury nodded. He was watching her closely.

"Well," she said, looking down again, "this is . . . awfully embarrassing. See, I thought the documentary was wonderful. I still do. And because I've always wanted to be a journalist myself, right after I saw Ms. Bromfield's film, I sent her my paper and a letter." Dee stopped and waited.

"What kind of a letter?"

"Oh"—Dee waved a hand dismissively—"it was . . . just a fan letter, really. But I asked her a couple of questions in it too."

"What did you ask her?"

"Well, I wanted to know where she'd gotten that

picture of Kate as a young girl. I'd never—"

"What'd she say?" Jury broke in. "Where'd she tell you she got it?"

"Well, that's the point. She never wrote back. I guess she thought that my paper was . . . well, childish, I suppose."

Jury didn't say anything, but Dee could feel him appraising her.

"What else did you ask her?"

"I wanted to know where she'd gotten a copy of the guards' testimony to the prison board. I've read what was leaked to the press. But most of the testimony was never made public, and yet there she was quoting from it."

"And you never heard from her at all?"

Dee shifted uncomfortably. "She never wrote me a word. Not a word. It hurt my feelings."

For a moment Dee paused and avoided looking at him. Then she laughed. "I shouldn't really have said that I *know* Harry. All I did was send her a letter."

"You know her well enough, I'd say," Jury put in grimly. "Ms. *Angius in herba.*"

"What? Do *you* know Harry?"

Jury cocked his head. "I think I know her pretty well. I too was impressed with her film. She has fine instincts for some things. I even thought for a while that we might research the Kate Soffel case together, but—" He stopped, as though reflecting. "Things did not work out," he said firmly.

When next he spoke, it was with brisk good humor. "Now see here, Ms. Diane Armstrong," he said. "The job of research assistant is yours if you want it."

"*If* I want it!" Dee exclaimed. "If—"

Jury held up a hand. "Always hear what the offer is first, Dee. Just let me finish. I want you to know I'm aware you're a college student. I know that you work as a waitress already and that you have a life of your own. But I think we can accommodate each other. I will need you only on the average of"—he waved a hand—"say, one day a week. A few hours one day a week, that is. We'll negotiate times, of course. Some of your work will be in conventional research, work in the library, checking records—all the sort of thing you've done before. But I'm also probably going to need you for . . . for some fieldwork as well."

"That's fine," Dee said.

"And I can pay you," Jury said, "a hundred and fifty dollars a month. Will that be acceptable?"

"Yes."

"Well then," he said. "It's settled." From the inside breast pocket of his sheepskin coat Jury withdrew an envelope. "For the rest of February," he said, handing it to Dee. "Beginning in March, payday will be every two weeks." Then he extended his hand to shake as she had offered hers earlier. It was a real handshake this time, though his hand was bony, as though she'd gathered up a bunch of spoons and forks from a dish drainer.

"And now, Dee Armstrong," Jury continued, "let me tell you what we're looking for. The diary, of course, but to find it, we first have to find where Kate is buried. I'd like you to make that your first priority."

Dee nodded. "All the obituaries say she was buried in Smithfield Cemetery. But if that were right, you'd have found her grave already, wouldn't you?"

"It's a complicated matter. If she's in Smithfield Cemetery, and I'm betting she is, the question is where, because there's no official record of her having been buried there. She died on August thirtieth, 1909, but the burial record of the Smithfield Evangelical Church—that was Kate's parish—lists no burial services performed at all between August twenty-seventh and September ninth. None. Nor do the cemetery records list a burial in that time period. There is a second record book at the church called the Book of Interments, which records the names of people from other parishes buried at the cemetery and also those from Smithfield who didn't have ordinary burial services: suicides, stillborn infants, and the like. But according to that book too, no interments of any kind took place at the cemetery between the twenty-seventh and the ninth."

"So they sneaked her into Smithfield somehow?"

Jury widened his eyes and cocked his head. "Four or five months ago I'd have said that that was impossible. You don't sneak people into cemeteries the way you sneak into a movie. But now I'm not so sure."

Dee pretended to think for a moment. She'd already considered a number of possibilities with Harry, of course. "Maybe the church recorded the burial under some other name—I mean other than Soffel or Dietrich or Miller."

"Dee, pay attention," Jury said testily. "*No* one, no one at *all,* according to any of the church records, was buried in Smithfield Cemetery between the dates of August twenty-seventh and September ninth. On the tenth a man named Havighurst was buried, and on the thirteenth someone else. Nothing in between."

"Okay. So she's in some other cemetery."

Jury nodded. "You'd think. But I checked every other cemetery in the city, every one still in existence, with no success. Of course, a lot of the old cemeteries are just gone now. A lot of others kept very sketchy records." He shook his head. "She *has* to be in Smithfield, though. I can't imagine that Gram—my grandmother—wouldn't have told me if she were somewhere else."

"What about the funeral director or the under-taker? Wouldn't he—?"

"They. Wouldn't they. Lutz and Beinhauer was the name of the firm, and it's still in business, though not under both names. Wouldn't they have a record of where Kate is? They certainly would, if their records still existed. But all the firm's records before 1952 were destroyed in a fire."

Dee and Harry had discussed one other possibility.

"Hey!" Dee said, pretending the idea had just come to her. "What about the hospital? She died at West Penn Hospital, didn't she?"

"Yes," Jury said with a smile, "and they undoubtedly have records that would help us. But they won't release them without a court order, which I have my reasons for not getting involved with. And in case you were thinking about a death certificate, I've checked into that too. The state will issue one only to a member of the immediate family or to a direct descendant."

"But you are a direct descendant, aren't you?"

Jury shook his head. "Not *direct*, no. The exact wording on the form refusing my request was that to get a death certificate you have to be 'a parent, grand-parent, spouse, brother, sister, child, guardian with a court order, or their legal representative.' Great half nephews, in other words, which is all I am, need not apply."

Dee took a deep breath and slowly let it out again. "So what do you want me to do?"

"I want you to find Kate's grave," Jury said simply. "I want you to begin by going over everything I've already been over. I don't think I missed anything, but it's best to be sure."

He paused a moment.

"And if we don't find anything in the records, I'll want you to check the names and dates on *every* gravestone in Smithfield Cemetery." He glanced up to the snow swirling outside the high-reaching window behind her. "You'll have to wait until the snow's gone, of course. Some of the headstones are set at ground level. Many have fallen over. It's quite an old cemetery."

Evidently that was what Jury had meant by field-work. "Do you think she was sneaked in there, then?"

He rubbed his forehead. "What I'm hoping is that there's a gravestone in the cemetery that, for some reason, neither the church nor the cemetery has a record of. I'll also want you to make a note of all the people buried under the names of Soffel, Dietrich, and Miller, and I'll want to know their exact locations. And finally, I'll want to know the name and location of anyone who was buried on the last day of August or during the first two weeks of September in 1909, no matter what name they were buried under."

"Wow! How big is Smithfield?"

"There are about twenty-eight acres of graveyard, but only about half of that is . . . tenanted, as you'll see. I don't know how many actual bodies there are. Also, you'll have to bear in mind that Kate's grave may be marked very minimally, with but a single name. Katherine perhaps, or Katrina, as Gram called her."

"They could bury people that way?"

"They could *mark* a grave that way; burials they were fussier about. How a grave was marked was left to whoever had bought it—and it was done at his or her expense. In fact, those who purchased the plots were not obligated to mark a grave at all if they didn't want to, at least in most cemeteries."

"So Kate could be in an unmarked grave?"

"We have to face that as a possibility, but again, I cannot imagine Gram not having told me a thing like that."

Dee studied Jury's tarry-looking coffee; he hadn't touched it that she could see. "Would it be okay with you if I had some help in this search? From two people, actually, two friends of mine. You won't have to pay them anything. I mean, I'd share what you give me with them. And I understand you'll probably want to interview them first."

For a while Jury stared at her, his face expressionless, and then he smiled. "I take it," he said, "that you are referring to your roommate, Megan, and"—he very deliberately leaned slightly to one side of Dee to look directly toward the rear of the coffee shop—"your young man, Cory?"

Dee felt herself blush. "You do your homework, sir," she said. God, she thought, he knew as much about her as Harry did. And now she was going to have to deal with the two of them.

Jury either coughed briefly or chuckled. "My dear good woman," he said, "surely you do not think I would have taken you on as my assistant without knowing any more about you than whatever you might have chosen to tell me this evening? After all, you yourself made preparations for our meeting"—Jury looked again in

Cory's direction and this time inclined his head in greeting—"did you not? For both of us, that is, *cucullus non facit monachum,* yes?"

It made her grin. An old guy he may have been, but he was no fool. "What's the Latin? What are you forcing me to say yes to, exactly?"

"Not 'force,' my dear. Never 'force.' The Latin might be rendered without gross inaccuracy as something like 'a cowl doesn't make a monk,' which in this case means—"

"I think I see what it means in this case. We're both from Missouri, right?"

"We seem to be, Dee. We seem to be. Incidentally, please feel free to take both Megan and Cory with you on the search, and I will not need to interview either one of them. Old-timer that I am, my work with young people for forty-five years has taught me something. You are not someone who would have rubbishy friends."

"Thank you," Dee said. And then she leaned forward earnestly. "Listen, Mr. Hammond. I have one more question I'd like to ask you, if it's all right." It would be wonderful, Dee thought, to bring Harry back something she didn't know.

He looked at her shrewdly. "Ask any question you like."

"Why didn't you start looking for the diary right after your grandmother died? What made you wait so long?"

Jury looked thoughtful. After a time, he shook his head and said, "Well, one thing I can tell you: I didn't at first know whether to believe Gram or not. Maybe there

94

was no diary. Maybe what I'd listened to in the hospital was only the raving of a . . . a delirious old woman." He stared down at the table, sucked in his lower lip, and seemed about to say something else, but he didn't.

"Yes," Dee said, "but what finally made you—?"

"I think that's enough for now," he said in a way that closed the topic absolutely. Then, as if remembering something, he reached down and brought his briefcase up from the floor. "Here, Dee," he said, extracting a manila envelope. "This is a present. In it you'll find a copy of the photograph of Kate as a young woman that you asked Ms. Bromfield about. Your paper made me think you might like it. Gram gave me my copy—and gave me to understand that it was the only one extant. Where Ms. Bromfield got hers, she would never tell me."

"I very much wanted a copy of that picture," Dee said. "Thank you."

"I also own a copy of the full testimony to the prison board about the escape. It's interesting primarily as an illustration of the conflicting opinions about Kate and her husband. I'll photocopy it for you."

Again, Dee thanked him. Was it from Jury that Harry had gotten her copy?

"And now, my dear," Jury said, "might be a good time for you to invite the excellent Cory to join us. Perhaps the two of you will allow me to indulge you in some of that magnificent-looking pastry. And we have plans to make, yes? *Tempus Fugit.*"

CHAPTER 9

For two weeks Dee and Megan rechecked all the records that Jury and Harry had been through already. They found nothing, no trace of a Kate or a Katrina or a Katherine Soffel or Dietrich or Miller who had been buried anywhere in Pittsburgh in 1909. Out of eagerness to move forward, Dee had quit her part-time job, but the weather and midterm exams postponed the start of their fieldwork for another week still. Finally, a brief thaw took away most of the snow, though it quickly turned cold again, and spring vacation from classes began.

It was Monday morning, the first day of vacation, and Cory, as usual, was late. Dee had agreed to pose for him at 9:00 A.M. Megan was due back around noon from a weekend visit with her family, and the three of them were to have lunch at the apartment and then pick up Jury for their first trip to Smithfield Cemetery.

But here it was, nearly 9:45, and Cory still hadn't arrived. Dee was disappointed but also angry, both at him and at herself for being angry. Cory was who he was, after all—and she'd already had ample indication of what that meant.

Last spring, still numbed by her parents' sudden divorce just a few months earlier, she'd been walking home from school alone in a light foggy drizzle, carrying an umbrella she never bothered to open. All of a sudden, from the center of a bed of blooming daffodils on the median strip of McPherson Boulevard, Cory sat up like a jack-in-the-box and pointed at her.

"You're Dee Armstrong and I'm Cory Windhover. I've been waiting for you. I think you're one of the most beautiful women I've ever seen, and I want you to pose for me."

Dee stopped walking and just stared at him. She knew who he was, of course, though the two of them had never spoken. He'd been two years ahead of her at Mellon High before dropping out at the start of his senior year to try to make a living as an artist. Everyone agreed he had talent. Maybe that was the reason he had so many girls buzzing around him—it sure wasn't his looks; he was as homely as a mud pie. He was also a real oddball. Sometimes he painted his fingernails. Now and then he wore rings in his eyelids. Dee remembered him being sent home from school once for sitting in the lunchroom eating bulbs of garlic as though they were apples. The last she'd heard of him was that he'd left home to live at an artists' co-op in the east end of Pittsburgh called The Colony.

"I know who you are," she said, walking again.

"Wait a minute," he said, scrambling to his feet and hurrying over to her. "I don't mean without your clothes on or anything like that."

His eyes were wide, hazel, and wondering—or maybe worried. He was six or eight inches taller than she was, rail thin, and he had shoulder-length matted blond hair. There was nothing in the least menacing about him. In fact, his long face looked to Dee like that of an old and patient horse. He had a daffodil in one hand, which he held out to her mechanically, as though he were returning something he'd borrowed, and which she accepted in the same mechanical way.

"You don't even know me," Dee said.

"Oh, yes I do," he said, laughing and showing a lot of big square teeth. "I knew you at school. I knew who you were anyway. I used to look at you. And I watched you ice-skate with Megan last winter at the pond in the park. I went up there especially to see you."

It gave Dee a queer feeling. Ice-skating was the only outdoor athletic activity that she really enjoyed, and she and Megan had been at the pond in Frick Park almost every weekend. He'd been there watching her?

"How come I never saw you?"

"I made sure you wouldn't. I didn't want you to think I was . . . you know."

"Why didn't you speak to me?"

He shrugged and laughed self-consciously. "Oh, . . . you know." He had on a jeans jacket over a T-shirt. Both looked soaked through, and he was shivering. "I'm not very good with words."

"You're going to catch cold," she said. "What's this posing stuff?" There was something childlike about him, innocent.

"Oh, well, all you have to do is sit. Well, you have to feel too, but you already do that. I'll show you. We can use the art room down in the basement at Mellon. Ms. Sorensen, you know? She likes my stuff and gave me a key. We can only be in there from five to six, though."

The rumor, Dee knew, was that Ms. Helga Sorensen, the very attractive head of the art department at Mellon High School, had cared about Cory as more than just a student. Of course, people like Cory invited rumors.

"Why don't you get Ms. Sorensen to pose for you?"

"Because," he said, very simply, "she's only pretty. I've drawn a lot of pretty girls. But you're beautiful."

Under ordinary circumstances, Dee's certainty of all that was wrong with the way she looked would have shut the door on Cory immediately: how her lips were too full and her breasts too small; her knees were too knobby and her nose all wrong; her hair was straight as a string and she was mousy. Mousy, mousy, mousy forever. But nothing about her life was ordinary at the time. Also, no one had ever called her beautiful before, not even her mother or father.

She started to walk again, and he fell in alongside her. "What's the difference between pretty and beautiful?" she asked.

He walked for a while thinking about it. "Well," he said, very much in earnest, "beautiful, see, is sort of a holy thing. You have to get inside to see it. But you can't *always* see it, because what's beautiful isn't always beautiful. Sometimes it isn't even pretty. A lot of times it isn't."

"Double-talk," she said.

"No! No! It isn't. It's me, how I'm saying it. I told you I wasn't any good with words. I'll just have to show you. I know I can show you."

There was a kind of certainty in his tone that she found compelling and unsettling at the same time. Again, she just stared at him.

He ran a hand impatiently through his soaking hair, muddy at the back from the flower bed. "See," he said, "*you* need to know this. About yourself, I mean. You don't know it now."

Her confusion disturbed her. "What do you mean?" she cried out, surprised to find herself close to tears. "I don't know what you mean!"

He took her arm. "Look," he said. "Let me have a

chance, will you please? I just have to have a chance to draw you."

He wasn't coming on to her, she was convinced. It was something else. And so she'd agreed to pose for him, and all last spring Cory had drawn her, and all summer, and this past fall—at first only in the basement art room at the high school, where everything smelled of chalk and turpentine and in a strange way blood, but then outside in the green air, and then everywhere, anywhere. She posed for him any way he wanted her to.

Simply staying still for twenty minutes was something she'd had to learn how to do—twenty on, twenty off, twenty on worked best for them both—but there were difficulties for Dee beyond the merely physical. Flattered as she was by Cory's attention, there was something eerie about being the object of such intense scrutiny, particularly when she was trying to focus on feeling what he asked her to: anger, calm contentment, sadness. All of what Megan called Cory's geekiness fell from him when he got absorbed in drawing, and at times Dee felt as though she were being observed by something larger than he was and as though she no longer knew who the two of them were. The feeling frightened but also excited her.

Once, early in their relationship, after he had worked a full session doing a study of her in charcoal, Dee had gone over to look at what he'd done. It bewildered her, the lines, the cross-hatching, the shadings and whorls, in the middle of which she seemed to sense rather than to see anything she would call herself.

"I thought maybe you'd—" She stopped.

"Maybe I'd what?" he asked her, his tone defensive.

All of a sudden she was shy, out of her depth, it felt like. "Don't you . . . do an outline or something? I thought that's what a study was, like a sketch." She caught her lower lip with her teeth and gestured at what he'd done. "It's as though you don't know me."

"Well, I don't, in a way. That's the point."

She looked down at the paper, frowning.

"Look," Cory said, "what I *don't* want is to see you just the way everybody else sees you—or even the way you see yourself. That's not how you're beautiful. I want to get *under* all that. I want . . ." He laughed in frustration. "I don't know how to say it. Maybe you'd better not look at . . . I mean, maybe you ought to wait till I finish something before you look at it." She'd never looked at any of his work in progress again.

Gradually Dee had come to realize that it wasn't just Cory's frustration with words that gave him trouble explaining what he was doing. He himself did not understand very well what was driving him or exactly where he was going when he was in the middle of something.

Nonetheless, in the beginning, just being with Cory, being along on his journey, had meant everything to Dee. She'd kept the daffodil he'd given her without ever telling him—or Megan either—pressing it in her dictionary and then putting it in a box with a few other things she meant to keep for the rest of her life. Being Cory's model had been a new identity for her, a new life. Maybe it was something like this Kate Soffel had felt because of the outlaw Ed Biddle.

But as adventuresome as it was being Cory's model, Dee was becoming increasingly conscious that she wanted more. In two months he'd be twenty-one, able, as he jokingly said, "to walk legally into any bar in the city." The reminder had disturbed her, even though she was perfectly aware that Cory didn't like bars, even though he seemed largely indifferent to the women he attracted without even trying to. Dee wanted him to stay interested in her, wanted to keep him interested in her by being someone interesting. Her prize paper, her decision to become a journalist, and now her work with Harry were all ways of ensuring that.

A staccato rap on the apartment door made Dee jump slightly, but then she had to smile at Cory standing silently before her in the doorway, an enormous paper folder obscuring him from the waist up, making him look like a box with legs.

She knew without his telling her that it was his pencil drawing of Kate as a young woman inspired by the photograph both Harry and Jury had given her.

"Go sit down on the couch," he said, grinning and

coming into the apartment. Dee sat down while he went to the bookcase on the other side of the room, slid out of his hooded sweatshirt, and extracted a large sheet of paper from the folder. He then leaned the folder carefully up against the bookcase and went over to Dee with his drawing. When he was seated beside her, he turned the paper over quickly and lay it across their knees.

"Careful," he said. "This is the original."

It was indeed the drawing of Kate she'd thought it was, and it was an astounding piece of work, teasing the eye as did an optical illusion, throwing one's attention first to one perspective and then to another. The luminous, spiritually intense face of the photograph had become gauzy and transparent, as though made of mist. It filled the page. But inside the face, swirling and receding as within a whirlpool, were a number of smaller faces, all likenesses of Kate but at seemingly different ages and reflecting different emotional states of being: grief, rage, desire, defiance, and so on. It wasn't possible to say whether the smaller faces were being sucked down into or thrust up from some black, unknowable abyss—and Dee knew that that was part of Cory's intention.

"Oh, my," she said involuntarily.

"That bad?" Cory asked, but of course he knew what she meant.

She pulled his head toward her and kissed his

cheek through his hair. "It's wonderful, Cory. It's really . . . powerful, staggering." She meant it too, even as she was conscious of the conventionality of her words. It didn't matter, though. Cory never wanted much conversation about his work.

She looked down at the drawing again. "Now, *she's* beautiful, isn't she?"

"Of course," he said. "I mean, I want her to be seen that way. She's lots of beautiful people—same way you are. And some ugly ones too."

"I can't wait till Megan sees it, and Jury."

"Jury already has. I dropped off his copy on my way over here."

She felt a stab of hurt. So that was why Cory had been late. Jury's house was between her apartment and the co-op where Cory lived, and he had stopped by once or twice to keep him posted on how the research was going and also to talk about art. They were becoming friends of a sort. Still, it wounded her that Cory had shown him the drawing first.

"Did he like it?" she asked without looking at him.

"He did. He said so—and so did his expression."

"Did he say it in Latin?"

"No," Cory said, laughing. "He quoted Shakespeare, I think."

She smiled slightly, looking down at the drawing. Cory kissed her, but then he drew back. "What's wrong?" he asked.

"Ohhh," Dee said in exasperation with herself. "Don't pay any attention to me."

He put the drawing gingerly on the coffee table and held her. And then he kissed her again. "Tell me," he coaxed.

"It's okay," she said. "Really. It's okay—just so Megan and I get a copy too."

"Hey. What do you think? I wanted you to see the original, but I had five copies made. I have yours matted already over in that folder."

"Could I . . . have one for my mom when I go down to see her? I can always show her mine, of course, but . . ."

"Sure," he said. "If you think she'll let it in the house."

"You know Mom doesn't feel that way about you."

"I know. Just Dad does," he said, laughing.

"He's protective is all, of his baby girl. Mom's a real fan of yours, Cory. Remember, she has a blown-up copy of the newspaper photo of *Woman in the Window* hanging in her dining room—and she's the one who had it blown up and framed."

"Yeah," he teased, "but she did that because the paper said you'd posed for it. Actually, you're the one she's the fan of." He put his arm around her. "Understandably, of course. I am too."

Dee thought *Woman in the Window* was the best drawing Cory had ever done of her. A photo of it had appeared in a Sunday supplement section of the

Tribune-Review devoted to a review of young artists in Pittsburgh, and the article had indeed named Dee as the model. It was a picture of the bare back of a young woman, of just her back and shoulders and head, looking out a window at a landscape. Remarkably, however, she seemed caught at precisely the moment she was turning to respond to something behind her. The drawing had awed Dee. It was some additional dimension of her that Cory seemed concerned with expressing, as though he were trying to render the aroma of a flower.

When Dee's mother had told her over the phone how much she liked the drawing, she did so in a way that implied she wanted to know more about Cory and their relationship. Dee gave a general outline of things, which was how her mother always seemed most comfortable with the events of her daughter's life anyway. At any rate, she hadn't hassled her about Cory after that. Dee's father, on the other hand, had nothing against Cory personally, Dee was to understand (she had assured both her parents that Cory wasn't into drugs or anything comparable and that he worked steadily), but his incomplete education and his hand-to-mouth existence didn't argue well for the future. Had Cory ever thought of art school? Was there any way the co-op where he lived and worked might get a group health plan of some sort? Perhaps Cory would be interested in a teaching position somewhere. And so on.

Dee took Cory's arm from around her and held his thick-fingered hand in her lap. The blunt strength of his hands reminded her of earth. Rich, dark, fertile earth. He shaped worlds with those hands, but she had no way of explaining what that meant to her to either her mother or her father.

"I have one other favor to ask of you. Would you give me a copy for Harry to see too—even if it's only for a loan?"

She felt him stiffen slightly. When Harry had taken the two of them, along with Megan, to dinner at a fancy French restaurant up on Mount Washington, they'd all been polite, but no one had had a very good time. Harry had continued to call Megan "Meeegan," even after being corrected.

"It really would be a favor, Cory. I know you don't like her much."

At dinner Harry had praised *Woman in the Window* by calling the drawing "interesting." Cory absolutely hated to hear any work of art referred to as "interesting" or "exciting."

He sighed heavily. "It isn't that I don't like her. It's . . . well, she's a little much, if you know what I mean."

Dee wasn't sure she did. "How do you mean?"

Cory fidgeted without answering.

"Do you think she's sexy?"

"Oh, yeah," he said. "I suppose she's that, all right."

And then he added, "I guess she can have a copy, if you really want."

Dee reached her head up to kiss him. "Thank you," she said. "I know you're doing it for me. It's just that I'm proud of you, Cory."

They nestled, just staying close. After a time Dee glanced down at her watch and said, "We don't have a lot of time before Megan gets here, but there's enough for you to have at least one session if you still want me to pose."

"Well," he said, his face flushed from being close to her. "Okay. Sure."

She turned away, as she always did, to slip off her sweatshirt and bra before sitting on the white sheet Cory draped over the couch. He sat on the floor across the room, drawing her in charcoal, his favorite medium. Hearing the scritch of the charcoal stick on the paper, watching him purse his lips to reflect on what he was doing, noticing the way he cocked his head first one way and then the other, Dee could feel herself vanishing and becoming real for him simultaneously—in the same way, it suddenly occurred to her, he did for her sometimes, as maybe everybody did for everybody, and maybe more than just some of the time.

CHAPTER 10

The twenty-eight acres of Smithfield Cemetery were spread over several gently rolling hills in a quiet corner of Pittsburgh known as Squirrel Hill. Megan drove slowly through the open iron gates of the main entrance and wound her way up to a spot from which the whole cemetery was visible. Off to the right, down at the side entrance, was a small stone office building. To the left, at the top of another hill, was a quaint twin-towered structure—a tiny church, it appeared to be—almost completely covered with ivy. And in between were the graves, row upon row of them, marked with every imaginable kind of headstone.

"That's the old Berg Memorial Chapel," Jury said in his raspy voice, pointing toward the building with the towers. "I think, Megan, it would be a good idea to park in front of it. We'll start our search in that area just to the right there."

The road inside the cemetery circled and back-tracked and ran into other small roads, but eventually Megan found a blacktop lane that took them in front of the chapel, where she parked. The snow was gone except for a few isolated pockets here and there, but an unfriendly March wind was blowing and there was no sun whatsoever. All four of them did up their coats the moment they got out of the car.

Dee had never actually walked the grounds of a cemetery before, and her response to Smithfield sur-prised her. With the possible exception of the old chapel, there was nothing spooky about the place at all. Its rows of headstones, in fact, upright as soldiers marching in lines across the closely cropped grass, had an artificial feel, as did a garden store's display of lawn ornaments. An instant cemetery, it seemed to Dee, like a scene from a pop-up book or the set for a movie.

The chapel, though, had a personality. Cory looked up at it with a low whistle of wonder. "Hey, hey, hey," he said in a soft voice, and then after a moment he said it again. He and Dee walked toward the building but could get no closer than about ten yards or so from the front doors. The dried stalks of a lot of bamboolike weeds taller than Dee's head choked the flagstone path to the entrance; several of the stones themselves had been pushed up by gnarled roots. Ivy sealed everything, obliterating all but the outline of the stone steps that led up to the two peaked wooden doors and binding the doors themselves from handle to hinge. It closed off most of the narrow mullioned windows and had reached above them to lace shut even the wooden louvers at the tops of the two towers. A number of the roof slates were missing, and some ugly holes had been eaten through the eaves straight into the building. What had seemed picturesque and fetching from a distance was pathetic up close, like the hopeful face of an abused child. Dee took Cory's arm, and they went back to Jury and Megan.

"Terrible, isn't it, the way the place has been let go?" Jury said. "The chapel's condemned now, the management told me. They'll just pull it down one day."

"They probably didn't use it for anything more than burial services," Cory offered. "It couldn't hold more than thirty people."

"I'll bet there are rats in it now," Megan said.

"Wouldn't you love to see inside it, though?" Cory exclaimed, walking over to look at the building from the side. "Are there pews and an altar and stuff like that still in there, do you think? Maybe there're bells in those towers."

"I read once where rats in cemeteries get the size of cats," Megan said. "They live on—"

"Megan!" interrupted Dee in a sharp whisper. She glanced over quickly at Jury. "Remember what we're here for. What's the matter with you?"

"All right now, people," Jury said, as though he were talking to a roomful of students. "May I have your attention, please? All of you have your notepads and something to write with? Your trowels and the plot plan?" Jury had bought each of them a blue spiral notebook, several different colored ballpoint pens, and a small trowel for cleaning earth off inscriptions. They were to share the plot plan, a single sheet as large as a road map when it was unfolded, showing the whole cemetery divided into areas marked by letters and, inside them, the location of every burial plot. "We will begin today," he said, pointing off to the right, "with the graves in areas G and F, extending from the side of the chapel to the fence over there at Aylesboro Avenue. Do *not* cross the blacktop road to go down to another section until we have completed sections G and F, if you please, and until we have conferred about how to move next."

Jury then went on to repeat what he'd already told the three of them in the car on the way over. With their black pens, they were to write in their notebooks *exactly* what was recorded on any headstone of any woman with the last name of Soffel, Dietrich, or Miller, no matter when the woman had died, and they were to mark the locations of such graves on their plot plan. In red, they were to mark the location of any man, woman, or child who'd died in the summer of 1909. And finally, with their green pens, they were to make a note of the location of any grave with a headstone that they could not read—because it was broken, for example, or weathered to illegibility. He was intending, he said, to check all the names and locations that Dee and Cory and Megan supplied him with against the information on the yards and yards of printout that the cemetery computers had fed him. Dee felt as though the three of them, to him, were little more than computers themselves.

They were about to set out when Jury told them to wait. "There's someone watching us," he said, pointing. "I saw him go behind that mausoleum down there."

"There's no rule against our being in here now, is there?" Megan asked.

"Don't be ridiculous," Jury said. "Of course not." And then he called out, "Hi there! You! Behind the mausoleum! Show yourself!"

Sure enough, a head full of fiery red hair poked out from behind the structure and then quickly ducked back.

"Come out, sir!" Jury cried again. "Come out! You will not be harmed! We wish only to talk with you!"

The head darted out again, a bit farther this time, but again it vanished. And then a head and an arm appeared, which also vanished. By degrees, a man emerged. He was short and broad with a mass of hair hanging loose about his shoulders and all but obscuring his face.

"Good heavens!" Jury exclaimed. "It's a troll. Come

up, please," he called. "We won't hurt you."

In fits and starts, with Jury several times having to encourage him, the man trudged up the hill. He dragged a half-full black plastic garbage bag behind him that clinked faintly when he was in motion. About five yards from Jury, he stopped and looked up. His face was lumpy, as though it had been beaten out of a sheet of metal, but smiling.

"I know a riddle," he said.

Jury's response was immediate but not one Dee would have predicted, not in a million years. "Do you really!" he said spiritedly. "Will you share it with us?"

The man ducked his head and snickered into his hand. Then, dropping the end of the garbage bag, he clasped both hands behind his back, struck a declamatory pose, and asked, "Who builds even better than the brick layer, the boat maker, and the carpenter?"

Jury looked at him with a slow knowing smile. "This riddle wouldn't have two answers to it, by any chance, would it?"

"It could," the redheaded man admitted with a cackle and a wide grin. He had no teeth.

"Aha," Jury said. "I see. All right, then. All right. Now, just let me think a moment." He then looked up at the sky, screwing his face into a parody of concentration. Then he frowned down at the ground. The troll bobbed his head delightedly. Dee glanced at Megan and at Cory, both of whom were grinning, as she was.

"How about . . . the grave maker," Jury said. "*He* builds better than those others."

The man's face fell but then almost immediately came to life again. "Why, though? Have to say why."

"All right," Jury said. "Now, don't tell me. Don't tell me." He studied the ground in front of him, elbow cupped in one hand, his chin resting in the other. The man rocked from side to side, grinning in excitement.

"How about this?" Jury said, as though the idea had just come to him. "The grave digger builds better because *his* houses last till doomsday. Is that right?"

The man's face absolutely crumbled, and for a moment Dee thought he was going to cry.

"But wait a moment!" Jury cried. "Wait a moment! I've been racking my brains for the *other* answer. Who *else* builds even better than the brick layer, the boat maker, and the carpenter? *Nobody* could know the answer to that riddle. *Nobody* could know."

"Yes, yes," the man said, his face breaking into a wide grin. "Old Jerry knows. It's the gallows maker, that's who."

"Have to say why," Jury said.

"Because," Jerry said, coming up on tiptoes, "because what he builds outlives a thousand tenants. Old Jerry knew! Old Jerry knew!" He pushed his hair up from his face, but almost immediately it fell back again.

"Jerry!" Jury said. "That's you, is it?"

"Jerry Giraffe," the man said, nodding his head rapidly.

"Giraffe?" Jury asked. "Like the animal?"

Jerry ducked his almost neckless head and then again nodded it up and down, up and down. "Ain't that a hoot?"

"Jerry Giraffe," Jury said. "Well, my name's Jury and I'm proud to know you."

"Judge and Jury," Jerry said emphatically. "Judge and Jury Giraffe."

Megan giggled.

"No, not *Judge* and Jury. Just Jury. And it's Jury *Hammond.*"

"Jerry Giraffe," Jerry said, pointing at his own chest. "Judge and Jury Giraffe," he insisted, pointing at Jury. "Ain't that a hoot?"

"Sounds like the Marx Brothers," Megan said, and the four of them laughed, which made Jerry laugh too.

"Judge and Jury Giraffe it is, then," Jury said. "Did you know that the riddle you told comes from Shakespeare? You were quoting from the graveyard scene in *Hamlet.* Did you know that?"

Jerry stared uncomprehendingly up through his matted red hair and shrugged.

"You work here, do you, Jerry?" Megan asked.

Jerry picked up the end of the garbage bag again and jounced it up and down. "I clean. Keep graves neat. Sometimes I dig." Again he pushed the hair out of his face, and again it fell right back.

"Say, Jerry," Jury said to him, "look at this." He stepped over to Dee. "May I use you as a model for a moment, my dear, to illustrate something to our excelent Mr. Giraffe?" He took her by one arm and turned her around. "See this," he said to Jerry, showing him the way Dee's ponytail was gathered at the nape of her neck. "Would you like an arrangement like this for your hair?"

Jerry came up close behind Dee and peered at her neck. Then he went over to look at Megan, whose hair was done in a braid. It was the braid he pointed to while looking questioningly at Jury.

"You want the braid," Jury said with a laugh. "Well, nothing's too good for a man who can quote Shakespeare. I used to braid my grandmother's hair. I hope I remember how." He took two rubber bands from his pocket and held them in his mouth. Then he turned Jerry around as he had Dee, swept his hair back, and went to work making the braid. Jerry's hair was filthy. Dee wouldn't have wanted even to touch it. But Jury worked adroitly and seemingly without distaste.

"That's a nice tight braid, Mr. Hammond," Megan said, nodding approvingly at what he'd done. "I'll let you do mine anytime you want."

"Megan, really!" Jury said, but Dee saw him smile.

"Say, Jerry," Cory said, pointing to the chapel, "is there any way in there?"

Jerry was happily flipping his braid first around to one side of his face and then to the other. "Oh, no," he said. "Just for hawks. Hawks and owls."

"Hawks and owls? You mean they live inside the chapel?"

"Up in the ivy," Jerry said. "They eat pigeons."

"Wow!" Cory exclaimed. "Right here in the middle of the city. Is that ever neat. Have—"

"All right now, everybody," Jury said. "Let's get to business. It's cold here and I'm going to wait in the car. Please bring me your first report in about an hour so I can check what you find against these confounded printouts. Megan, you'd better give me the keys in case I get colder still and need the heater. Jerry, I expect you have your own work to do, though you may certainly accompany my trusted lieutenants here if you wish or, should you get cold, come sit in the car with me. We are looking, Jerry, for the resting place of an ancestor of mine named Katherine Dietrich or Katherine Soffel or Katherine Miller. Would you happen to know of such a grave?"

"Katherine Giraffe," Jerry said solemnly, at which Megan giggled again.

"No, no. Katherine *Dietrich*, or *Soffel* or *Miller.* You wouldn't know where anyone like that is, by any chance, would you?"

"Dietrich Giraffe," Jerry said. "Soffel Giraffe. Miller Giraffe." He pointed at himself. "Jerry Giraffe." And then he pointed at Jury. "Judge and Jury Giraffe."

"That's all right, Jerry," Jury said, patting him on the shoulder. "My lieutenants are on the case, yes,

119

people? *Ex nihilo nihil fit,* yes? And *sovitur ambulando.* 'Let's get moving, please,' in the vulgar tongue."

All afternoon, as well as on the afternoons of Tuesday, Wednesday, and Thursday, the three lieutenants looked for Kate Soffel's grave. At first they found the variations in the shapes and types of grave markers fascinating. There were Greek crosses, they learned from Jury, Maltese crosses, Latin and patriarchal crosses. There were headstones six or seven feet long, made to resemble couches. Other headstones were topped with carved lambs or funerary urns or mourning cherubs. They saw bronze plaques, sometimes set directly into the ground, other times riveted into boulders. There were Masonic symbols, carvings of yew trees with drooping branches, and all kinds of carved angels.

They also learned more specialized cemetery terminology from Jury. "Footplates" were long narrow pieces of marble set flush with the ground before groupings of graves and were always inscribed with a family name or sometimes with several family names. More often than not, they were grown over with turf and had to be scraped clean with their trowels. A "stele" monument was not the same as an "obelisk." There were different kinds of mausoleums, and so forth. And finally, there were the exotic-sounding names and inscriptions on the headstones themselves, almost all in German, which Megan, who'd had two years of the language in high school, loudly pronounced for them, ripping out the shorter names in brief explosions of sound—Ertz, Zahl, Fiest—and making the longer ones rumble like freight trains—Katzenhabendeinst, Eichenlauberholz.

But as hour after hour of searching turned up nothing promising in the way of a lead to Kate's grave, the novelty of what they were doing began to wear off, and they became increasingly concerned that their survey was going to be as fruitless as their work rechecking the church and cemetery records had been. Cory spent a lot of time sketching the ruined chapel from different angles. Megan grumbled almost constantly about having to write down all the information Jury had requested: "What's he need it for? What's he going to do with it?" And Dee began to wonder whether the pathway to a career she'd been imagining for herself even existed.

She didn't feel as connected with Jury as Cory and Megan seemed to. The gaze of his crushed-ice eyes still froze something inside her. But she grew easier with him. All three of them, at his invitation, began to use his first name. On the second afternoon of their search, he brought along a couple of thermoses full of hot herb tea and a dozen homemade cinnamon muffins, which they shared among themselves and with Jerry. That same day, driving home, Megan had to brake hard for a large black cat at the cemetery gates. Jury remarked, with an absolutely straight face, on the arrogance of cemetery rats. "They can get to be the size of cats, you know, when they live on nothing but rotted corpses." Megan grinned and blushed, but the next afternoon after one of their tea breaks, she got out of the car and in a loud voice announced: *"Legiones Juriatum, haulen tukese!"*

"What's that?" Jury asked her with a sharp look. "Say that again."

Megan said it again.

Jury studied her and then after a time cleared his throat slightly. "My dear good woman," he said, "your pronunciation—"

"Is perfect," Megan interrupted airily, "if you know Latin. All I said was, in the vulgar tongue, 'Legions of Jury, it's time to haul ass.'"

Gradually they came to know a lot more of Jury's reasons for believing that Kate and the Biddles had been set up by a conspiracy. The guard who gave the most damaging testimony against Kate to the prison board, for example, by saying he'd seen her blowing kisses to the Biddles and flirting with them—this same Frank Chase, fired by the board for his ineptitude during the escape, later came into enough money from an undisclosed source to buy his own business. Had he been paid off? Similarly, Maggie Vogel, Kate's housemaid, who, days after the escape, found a love letter from Ed Biddle to Kate hidden under a carpet and who testified both to Kate's general profligacy and to her starry-eyed infatuation with the Biddles, also later received a sum of money from somewhere—enough to enable her to stop working and to marry one Mike Roach, the same Mike Roach, a streetcar conductor, who was one of the five men prepared to swear at Kate's divorce trial that he had had sexual relations with her. And Jury told them of instance after documented instance of Peter Soffel's weasely vindictiveness, his reputation for never forgiving either a slight or an error. He was just the kind of man who could deprive Kate of her children, if that were something he considered necessary to get what he wanted.

"I was sure when I wrote my paper that Kate had just abandoned her children," Dee said.

"Far from it," Jury said firmly. "Far from it."

"Do you think she ever saw them again?" Megan asked.

"Oh, I suspect she did from time to time—at the train station maybe or in some closely supervised location. Peter was too smart to have risked letting her see them alone, but he was also too smart to risk her concluding he was never going to let her see them at all."

"What a fourteen-carat gold-plated prick the guy was," Megan said, "if you'll pardon my Latin."

"Well," Jury responded dryly, "that's one way of putting it anyway. He seems to have been a man who believed that he was only what he owned, and that he could be no more than that. And so he tried to own a lot of things that simply can't be owned like a wife, children, affection, and respect. He wasn't alone in his belief, by any means, particularly in Pittsburgh. In fact, if you look at the careers of Carnegie, Frick, Mellon, and the rest, and look at their impact on the country, you might almost say it was the belief of America at the time."

He looked out his side window at the orderly rows of graves.

"Sometimes I think it still is," he added.

The thing Dee remembered most vividly from their four afternoons at the cemetery, however, was Jury's response to Cory's wondering why the location of Kate's grave should be such a mystery. "I mean, even at the time, there must have been people who thought she got a raw deal. You'd think *somebody* would have marked where she was with some kind of memorial."

Jury turned around from the front seat of the car saying, "No, no, no, no. Such a monument would have been instantly defaced, which is why the family was so secretive about the funeral arrangements. You have to understand that the story the press created about Kate, created with Peter's help, of course, was what most people thought had really happened, which means that she was not only hated but feared, feared as one might an infectious disease. She'd made a bargain with the devil, you see, taking up with those two boys the way she did, and she'd made it knowingly and willingly so far as most people were concerned. What people feared was that other wives and mothers would do what Kate did. They feared contagion, the beginning of a plague that would overthrow all civilization if it were allowed to spread."

"Yes," Dee said from the backseat. "A couple of newspapers even talked about her as having been kissed by a vampire."

"She'd done worse than that in the public's opinion," Jury said. "She'd kissed the vampire back. Did you know that the novel *Dracula* had come out in America only a few months before the Biddles' escape? I sometimes think one of the reasons it became as popular as it did was that it made clear how the vampire-kissed woman is an eroticized woman and how she is the destroyer of civilization."

"Somebody who needs a stake through the heart to restore her purity, I suppose," Megan said dryly.

"You joke, Megan, but it may interest you to know that when it was believed Kate would die from her bullet wound, a minister, up around Oil City somewhere, I believe, actually proposed that for the good of her soul as well as for the good of the community she be buried at a crossroad—after first being decapitated and staked through the chest."

By the middle of Thursday afternoon, Dee, Megan, and Cory had finished checking all the graves in the cemetery. They'd come up with only five totally illegible stones, the location of which they'd duly noted and reported to Jury. They'd also found markers for three Soffel women, eleven Dietrichs, and ten Millers, and though one of the Dietrich women had been born the same year as Kate, 1867, not one had died within four years of her death. They found seventeen people who had died in 1909, but none had been born in the year Kate was. If Jury had been able to make any use of any of the information they'd given him, he hadn't said so.

The three were gathered at the bottom of a slope hidden from Jury's view.

"So now what?" Megan asked.

"If Kate's here," Cory said, looking up over the gently undulating field of graves, "then she's got to be somewhere unmarked." They could all see that there were a lot of empty spaces in the rows of stones, gaping like missing teeth.

"Maybe," Dee said dispiritedly. "Or maybe she was buried under some other name, even though Jury thinks she couldn't have been. Or maybe a little elf snuck in here and changed both the name and the date on Kate's stone. Whatever, we're at a dead end."

"Unless Judge and Jury Giraffe has plans he hasn't told us about," Megan responded. "Let's go ask him."

CHAPTER II

"Yes, yes, Dee, of course Jury was 'crushed,'" Harry interrupted. "I mean, what did he *say* when you gave him the news? Try to remember what he said *exactly*. This is important."

The remarks were particularly withering coming over the phone, as though Harry were blaming Dee personally for their not having found anything at Smithfield. Dee cleared her throat and pitched her voice slightly lower to suggest she was calmer than she really was. "The only thing he said was, 'I was afraid of that.'"

"And on the way to his house? Or when you dropped him off?"

"Nothing."

"So he never said anything about what he was going to do next?"

"No. We asked him about it too. Megan did. But he didn't answer."

In fact, slumped in the front seat of Megan's car, Jury'd looked to Dee as though he didn't care whether he saw the next day.

"And all that information he had you collect for him he just threw away! Can you be a little clearer, please, about what you mean by 'just threw away'?"

The way Harry was repeating her words and phrases put Dee's teeth on edge.

"He scrunched up all those printouts and told that guy Jerry to put them in his trash bag."

"What about his notes? Did he throw them away too?"

Dee thought for a moment. "I don't think he did, no."

"How about *your* notes? Did he want them? Or your plot plan?"

No, Dee felt tempted to say, he was too busy describing the orgy to which we were all invited. More and more, she felt Harry was treating her like a child over these progress reports she was making. Or like a slave.

"No," Dee said curtly.

Harry didn't say anything for a time. And then she asked, "Did he have a plot plan of his own?"

"I assume so," Dee said. "Don't you think he would?"

Again, Harry didn't speak right away. And then

she said bitterly, "So it's all over, then, isn't it? Either that, or the old goat's already got what he was after. And then it's really over."

The words "old goat" grated on Dee. "What do you mean 'got what he was after'?" Let her see how she liked being quoted that way and questioned about it.

"You found him a lot of Miller graves, yes? Suppose his grandmother told him Kate was buried two unmarked graves over from the Miller stone in plot E or some such. You think that old fox wouldn't know how to act 'crushed' in front of you three?"

Dee's insides froze. It had never occurred to her that Jury could be tricking them. She felt like a fool.

"He's still going to need us, though, isn't he? At least if the diary's buried, he will."

Harry didn't respond for so long that Dee asked if she were still there.

"Yes. I'm sorry. I was thinking. Dee, I'm also sorry I was so abrupt with you. I just found out I have to leave town in the morning, and I've got a thousand things on my mind right now. Maybe it would be better for us to meet later. Could you? About nine . . . just for a half hour or so? I could pick you up and drop you back at your apartment."

"Okay," Dee said. "But at Hillman Library, all right? Not at the apartment. I have to do some stuff for school."

"At the library, then. Good. I'll pick you up at the main entrance at nine o'clock."

•   •   •

It was cold waiting outside the library, and Dee felt sick to her stomach. Was Harry just going to give up on the diary—or worse, give up on her?

Harry arrived a little before 9:00. "Oh, Dee," she said the moment Dee got into the car, "I am truly, truly sorry for the way I acted on the phone. I didn't mean to imply that you and Megan and Cory had done a bad job with Jury, because you haven't. I was just disappointed about Smithfield, as I know you are. I hope we're still friends, friend."

"Oh, sure," Dee said. "Forget it."

"No, Dee, no," Harry said, patting her leg. "I don't want to do that. I told you about me and rudeness. I was rude this afternoon, and I'm sorry."

Harry's car, a silver-gray BMW convertible, nosed through the shoals of Oakland traffic as smoothly as a cruising shark. It was warm inside and filled with soft music turned very low; it smelled of musk perfume, leather, and cigarettes. The car was just the sort Dee had imagined for Harry, and she drove it just the way Dee thought she would.

They wound their way up into Schenley Park and parked in a pull-off area. The cars on the parkway in the near distance flowed east and west like rivers of light. Three other cars were parked just down from them. Dee could see that the windows of the closest were steamed up.

"Auditions," Harry grinned, nodding at the other vehicles. "Thank God I don't have to do that anymore." Then she quickly added, "I hope you don't mind talking here. I thought it might be more private than going for coffee." She opened her window about six inches. "Would you mind terribly if I had a cigarette, if I promise to blow all the smoke out the window?"

"Fine," Dee said, though it wasn't. And then she added, "I didn't know you were going away. You're leaving tomorrow, you said?"

Harry nodded while lighting her cigarette. "As I told you, I didn't know it myself until today. Yes. I'm leaving in the morning and for more than the weekend, I'm afraid. I've got to go to California and then to Oregon to interview those female smoke jumpers I told you about. The station has finally decided to fund the story."

"Another TV special!" Dee said, though her heart sank. This was just the sort of thing she'd feared. "That's great, Harry!"

"Yes, it is. I've got a chance of being shown nationally with this one, my producer said."

"Wow! That's *really* wonderful. Congratulations." How was Harry going to stay interested in some phantom diary with the prospect of a national reputation in front of her?

"How long will you be gone?"

"Ten days at the least. Two weeks most likely."

Two weeks, Dee thought in despair. *Two weeks!*

"Now listen, Dee," Harry said crisply. "I want to talk about our next move."

"With finding the diary?"

"Of course. What else?"

Dee leaned back into the headrest and put a hand to her chest. Relief flooded warmly into her. "I'm just glad you don't want to . . . just forget about it."

"Not at all," Harry said, shaking her head and smiling. "Not at all. I think you're right that Jury's still going to need the three of you even if he knows where Kate's grave is now, which, after I thought about it, I can't believe he does. It's just like him to have had you collect the information you did—the location of everybody in Smithfield who died in the summer of 1909, for God's sake—without having any idea of what he was going to do with it." She chuckled. "The old goat just had to convince himself he was being thorough."

She tapped the ash of her cigarette out the open window.

"Mind you," Harry continued, "there's still a chance he's trying to con us, but I don't think there's much of one."

"So . . . ," Dee asked, "how *do* we move, then?"

Harry took a long pull on her cigarette, inhaled it, and then blew what she'd inhaled out her partially opened window. She threw the rest of the cigarette away, rolled up the window, and turned in her seat to face Dee directly.

"Kate's death certificate would tell us where she was buried."

Dee didn't say anything for a moment. "But Jury told me that only a direct descendant or a member of the immediate family or a lawyer could—"

"So what if we go through a lawyer?"

Dee just stared at her.

"You want to know why I think *Jury* never went through a lawyer?" Harry continued. "He didn't want to have the fact that he's a bastard and his mother a suicide dragged up in court, which it would have been, of course."

Dee couldn't believe Harry had used a term like "bastard" right along with what she'd said about Jury's mother. "His mother *killed* herself? Are you sure? It's not on the data sheet you gave me."

Harry shook her head. "No, it isn't. I thought maybe she'd died in childbirth, but I just found out what really happened." She grinned at Dee. "The story here gets better and better, doesn't it?"

It was too much for Dee to take in all at once. *How* had Harry just found out that Jury's mother had committed suicide? Did Jury himself know? It was as though Harry had lines out all through the city, like the threads of an enormous web. The Spider Lady indeed. Dee remembered Megan's saying once that she hoped never to be in the way of anything Harry wanted.

"But how could we get a lawyer to work for *us*? Isn't Jury the one who'd have to hire a lawyer?"

Harry took out another cigarette and tamped it on the dashboard. "Our hope, I think, is my station's lawyer. We may not even have to hire him, by the way. We're not trying for an exhumation order here, Dee. All we want is a death certificate. I'll see if I can get him to pull a few strings as soon as he gets back from vacation."

"He's on vacation?! When's he get back?"

"About the same time I do. Right around Easter."

It was an eternity. "That's even *more* than two weeks, Harry. What if you were right that Jury really did find what he needs to locate Kate's grave? Won't he get there long before we do?"

"He's still going to need you, just as you said. I think the diary would have to be buried. He's not going to dig it up himself."

Harry put the tamped cigarette in her mouth but then crumpled it in the ashtray. "Suppose you're the direct descendant of someone dead," Harry asked, as though addressing the question to the universe. "What exactly's involved in getting a death certificate for them? Did Jury say? Do you know?"

"He didn't, no, and I haven't a clue."

"Neither do I, though I should. Neither did anyone I talked to at the station earlier today. I mean, let's suppose you wanted a death certificate for your grandmother, or better still, your great-grandmother. And let's suppose you showed up in Pittsburgh from Philadelphia, say, and went to the Health Department here, or the Bureau of Birth and Death Records, or whatever it is, and said you were only going to be in town a day or so and you wanted a copy of your great-grandmother's death certificate so you could find where she'd been buried. You needed the information so you could go pay your respects at her grave. What would they do?"

Dee swallowed hard. "I don't know."

Harry looked out the windshield for a time. "They couldn't expect you to be able to prove it, could they, with a family Bible or something? But I don't think there's any way I could prove who my great grandmother was no matter what they wanted."

"I don't even *know* who my great-grandmother was."

Neither of them spoke for a time. Finally, Harry sighed and said, "I really should know the procedure. I'll make some phone calls as soon as I get back."

"I can do that," Dee said. "Now, I mean. Tomorrow."

Harry smiled at her. "Dee," she said, "let me do some legwork for a change. Anyway, your main job while I'm gone is to keep an eye on Jury. He'll certainly stay in touch with you all. Be friendly with him. Fuss over him. You know, take him for pizza or something."

"I can do all that and still find out how to get a death certificate. I don't have to use my name, you know, and I need the experience."

Harry looked at her and then smiled and nodded. She touched the tip of one finger gently to Dee's cheek. Dee felt a shock go through her.

"Okay, make some calls, then. Such an intense girl you are, Diane Armstrong. You remind me of me. Oh," Harry said, jumping slightly, "speaking of which . . ."

Harry then reached over her seat and picked up a new, leather attaché case from the back floor. "This is for you, colleague." She smiled at Dee.

"Really?!" Dee cried. "For me! Really?" She snapped the catches open and lifted the lid of the case. The inside of it smelled like a new world, like a promise she'd wanted someone to make to her the whole of her life.

"Well," Harry said, "we can't have you doing professional work from a backpack, now can we?" She glanced down at the dashboard digital clock. "Oh, my God," she said. "Look at the time." It was a bit past 9:30. "I've got a seven-thirty flight out in the morning, and I'm not even packed."

Harry started the car and backed out of the pull-off area. "Oh," she exclaimed, raising one hand. "Will you please tell Cory for me how much, how very, *very* much I like the drawing of Kate you gave me? And please let him know that I tried a number of times to get him at The Colony to tell him so directly. That's the truth too, Dee. The damned phone there is either busy or nobody answers."

"Oh," Dee agreed with a chuckle, "you don't need to tell me about trying to telephone The Colony. About the only way you can get somebody there is to pound on the door. And of course I'll tell Cory. He'll be really pleased."

"Would you tell him also that if I—I mean, *when* I do the special on Kate's diary, I'll want to use his drawing to frame everything? I like it that much. Maybe I'll be able to do something on The Colony too—at some later point, I mean."

As she drove toward Dee's apartment building, Harry asked, "Have your parents ever seen Cory's work?"

"Oh, sure," Dee said. "Mom likes his stuff a lot. I think she'll like the drawing of Kate as much as you do. I hope she does anyway."

"She will," Harry said emphatically. "Believe me. He draws like a god, this young man of yours. One thing I know is talent, and I've got a feeling your mother's probably the same way. An herbalist, is she?"

Dee nodded and then froze. She was sure she'd never told Harry anything about her mother, particularly that she was an herbalist.

"And you're still going down to see her Easter weekend?"

"Yes."

When Harry pulled up in front of Dee's building, she slid to a stop but kept the motor running. Then she took Dee's elbow.

"One more thing," Harry said. "You've got a second main job while I'm gone. I don't mean to sound like a mommy here, but you're going to have to start keeping up better with your schoolwork. You haven't been, you told me, right?"

Dee looked down without answering.

"It's important, Dee. And it's not that hard to do, not any harder than it is to get A's these days, and they're important too. They don't mean that much if you have them. They don't mean anything, really. But it means a lot if you *don't* have them. You follow me?"

"Yes," Dee mumbled without looking up.

"Okay, then," Harry said, punching Dee's jaw playfully. "You be all caught up by the time I get back. And make up your mind to get a four-point zero average this term.

"Now, look, we'll both be back in Pittsburgh about the same time. The night of Easter Sunday. Trust me to get to our station's lawyer the minute I get home. Jury's not going to walk away with anything, believe me. You can leave me a message if you need to on either of my machines. I'll check them every day."

Dee got out of the car and was heading for her apartment when Harry opened her window and called her back. She'd forgotten her attaché case.

• • •

At 9:00 the next morning, Friday, the last day of spring vacation, the first thing Dee did was to call the Birth and Death Records Subdivision of the Department of Health, listed just that way in the City and State Directory section of the telephone book.

"Oh, hello," Dee said. And then she began reading from the notes she'd written out for herself the night before. "My name is Brandy Stevens, and I wonder if you would be able to help me. I've just moved out here to Pittsburgh from Philadelphia, and I'm trying to locate the grave of my great-great-grandmother. Now, I know she died here of typhoid fever in August of 1909, but—"

"Oh, we wouldn't have her," the woman interrupted. Dee could hear her chewing gum.

"I beg your pardon?" Dee said.

"She's not here. She wouldn't be in here."

"But you don't even know her name yet. How can you be sure that—"

Again, the woman interrupted. "It don't matter what her name is. You say she died in 1909?"

"Yes."

"What are you after, a death certificate?"

"Yes."

"We only have records of people who died in Pittsburgh before 1906. You'll have to get in touch with the Division of Vital Records in New Castle. That's about fifty miles north of here. I can send you the form you'll need to fill out, if you want."

"Couldn't I just call them? I'd like to get the information as soon as possible so I'll have it for my family when they get out here."

"You could call, sure, but it won't do you no good. They don't give out information over the phone. Neither do we. Better let me send you the form."

"That would be great, then. Thank you."

"Okay. Now, it's Brandy Stevenson you said? That's your name?"

"Well," Dee said, glancing at her notes, "it's Brandy *Stevens*—but that's my maiden name. I forget I'm married sometimes."

The woman chuckled. "I know what you mean, honey. So what is your name, then, and where do I send this?"

Dee gave the woman the name Brandy Armstrong and the address of her apartment, thanked her again, and then asked if, by chance, she had the telephone number of the Division of Vital Records. "I figured I'd ask them what kind of proof I have to have," she explained.

"How do you mean, 'proof'?"

"Well, you know. Proof that I'm a direct descendant. Proof that my great-great-grandmother really was . . . or is . . . my great-great-grandmother. Won't they want me to prove that?"

"All you got to do is say how you're related and

sign the form I'm sending you. And come up with the three bucks, of course. There's a three-dollar charge."

"And that's it? That's enough? They'll give me a death certificate?"

"You can't just run the form up there and have them hand you one, if that's what you mean. This is a bureaucracy. But they'll mail one to you."

Dee couldn't believe it. All she had to do was say Kate was her great-great-grandmother and send in three dollars and she'd get back information that had eluded Jury and Harry—and Cory and Megan and herself—for weeks, months, maybe in Jury's case even years.

"Can you tell me one other thing, please?" she asked. "I'm not sure what name my grandmother was buried under exactly. It could have been one of three, so—"

"Your grandmother? I thought this was your great-great-grandmother."

"It is. Did I say 'grandmother'? I'm sorry. I *meant—*"

"You got the date and place of death?"

"Yes."

"Exactly?"

"Yes."

"They'll have her. They'll find her. The name don't matter."

From information, Dee got the telephone number of the Division of Vital Records in New Castle and listened to a long recorded announcement on how to obtain birth and death records, one so detailed and with so many options that she had to listen to everything twice and take notes. A request for a death certificate, the announcement said, had to include a letter giving the name of the deceased, the date and place of death, the requester's relationship to the deceased, the reason for the request, a self-addressed stamped envelope, the requester's telephone number, and a three-dollar payment in the form of a check or money order. No cash. Normally, Dee was told, the process took about eight weeks. But if the request was sent to the division by Priority Mail, it would be answered within five to ten days. The announcement said nothing about a form. So, Dee figured, maybe there was no need to wait for it.

She never gave what she was doing a second thought, and by the time she'd finished composing her letter she almost believed what it said:

Friday, March 27
Pennsylvania Department of Health
Division of Vital Records
P.O. Box 1528
New Castle, PA 16103-1528

Dear Sir or Madam:

I wish to visit the grave of my great-great-grandmother in order to honor her memory, and I am requesting a copy of her death certificate so that I may locate her burial site.

My great-great-grandmother was married several times. Her death certificate, therefore, may be in the name of Katherine or Katrina Miller, Katherine or Katrina Dietrich, or Katherine or Katrina Soffel. There is also a chance she is buried under still another name, but I am sure of the date, the place, and the cause of death. She was born July 26, 1867, and died August 30, 1909, of typhoid fever at West Penn Hospital, Allegheny County, Pittsburgh, Pennsylvania.

I am enclosing a self-addressed stamped envelope and a postal order for $3.00 to cover the cost of the certificate. I am mailing this Priority Mail.

Thank you for your kind and prompt attention to my request.

Sincerely yours,

Diane Armstrong
412-555-2087

All the way home from the Squirrel Hill Post Office and for the rest of the day, Dee tried to calm her excitement by telling herself not to count on getting what they needed. But she couldn't really make herself believe she wouldn't succeed. She felt fated somehow to get what she was after, as though she'd been chosen.

CHAPTER 12

Dee planned to leave for her weekend visit with
her mother on Good Friday—two weeks from the
day Harry left for the West Coast. After mailing her
letter to New Castle, she swore to herself she'd say
nothing to anyone about what she'd done until there
was something definite to report. She also swore to
herself (as well as to Cory, Megan, and Jury) that on
the day she left town, she'd be caught up on all her
schoolwork. These decisions focused her in much the
same way her work on her senior paper had in the
midst of her parents' divorce. She did go twice with
Cory and Megan to visit a deeply depressed Jury, once
with Chinese take-out, once with pizza, but the rest of
the time she spent studying, working straight through
even the private hours she and Cory ordinarily reserved
for each other.

Only once did she waver in her resolve. On Wednesday of the first week of Harry's trip, a blank application form to obtain a death certificate addressed to one Brandy Armstrong arrived at the apartment. Luckily, Dee was alone when the mail came. She quickly saw that the letter she'd sent had supplied all the information the form required: her relation to the deceased, her reason for requesting the death certificate, and so forth. But a statement under where she was to sign her name sent a tiny shiver up her back: "In accordance with Statute 4904, Unsworn Falsification to Authorities, I state that to the best of my knowledge all of the information supplied above is accurate." But tempted as she was to talk over what she'd done with Cory, Megan, and even Jury, Dee remained silent. What was done was done. She tore the form into pieces, buried them at the bottom of the kitchen wastebasket, and went back to writing her paper on *Middlemarch*.

Dee slept soundly during her two weeks of concentrated work, but she dreamed a lot. Busy dreams. Odd dreams. Dreams she could neither discard nor understand. They weren't nightmares, but they were just as hard to shake off because night after night certain images came back, of her mother and Kate mainly, but always in strange new contexts. In one dream, Kate appeared in blackface on a vaudeville stage. She was braying like a donkey while being applauded wildly by a number of women who all looked like Dee's mother and who were all wearing gingham dresses like Dorothy's in *The Wizard of Oz*. Another time, all the dolls and stuffed animals from Dee's childhood were sitting around half buried in a cow pasture, listening to Kate and Dee's mother trying together to play a duet on an enormous ruined organ.

Dee was aware that she had complicated feelings about her mother and knew also that her decision to see her again was almost certainly connected with the new Kate Soffel that Harry and Jury had given her to consider, but exactly how everything fit together involved questions she kept dormant by concentrating on her studies. On the way down to her mother's small farm in Megan's car, however, one question raised itself. Even before the divorce, there had always been something indistinct for Dee about her mother, not quite in focus somehow, as with a slightly blurred photograph, and she had concluded that her mother was not someone to rely on. But was Kate's story a confirmation of this position or a suggestion that Dee needed to rethink it?

Marie Armstrong now lived just outside a small farming community called Wolfdale, about thirty miles southwest of Pittsburgh, with a woman named Alice McClintock: slim, quiet, forty-something, with white-blond hair as fine as corn silk and eyes the most startling cobalt blue Dee had ever seen. Alice was Norwegian. She spoke English perfectly but with an accent. She had been a nurse at Shadyside Hospital when Dee's mother was hired there as an herbalist, the first the hospital had ever employed. The two became friends, and less than a month after Dee's father had moved to California, Alice had come to live with them in Pittsburgh.

At one time Dee had tried to blame Alice for her parents' divorce, though both parents denied she'd had anything to do with it. Dee couldn't say for sure that Alice and her mother were lovers. She'd never seen them kissing or anything like that; they hadn't shared a bedroom in Pittsburgh (and, to judge from her mother's letters, still did not). But when the closeness between the two women apparently became too much for their hospital supervisors—though the reason given for their being laid off was "downsizing decisions"—that became too much for Dee. If Alice were going to continue to live with them, Dee made clear, then right after high school graduation, she was going to live at Megan's until August, when the two of them would get an apartment near the university. Dee's mother said only that she was sorry, but that she understood.

The last time the two had seen each other was when Dee was picking up the remainder of her clothes to move to Megan's and had come into the kitchen unheard. Her mother was standing at the sink looking out the window above it, humming softly, and very slowly rubbing lotion on her hands. For a time Dee just stood and watched her, breathing in the delicate fragrance. It was a very special lotion her mother was using, one she created for only a few wealthy women from certain herbs and flowers. Dee had never known her to use it herself. Still rubbing her hands, Dee's mother had turned and, upon seeing Dee, jumped slightly.

"Oh, Dee," she said with a little laugh. "You startled me. I didn't know you were here."

A kind of darkness came into Dee's mind at that moment, and she reeled and almost fell. At the feel of her mother's arms around her, however, she shoved back hard, separating the two of them. "You're disgusting!" she cried.

"Why?" her mother said, her face white and horrified.

"Why?!" Dee almost screamed. "Why?"

And then she began to cry, sobbing at first. She'd cried until she was exhausted.

After a time, Dee heard her mother sit down at the kitchen table. "I know you're angry," she said, "and I can certainly guess some of the reasons. But I don't want to just guess. I'd like you to tell me what you're so very angry at, all of it, if you can—and if you will."

"Ha! As if you didn't know."

"Tell me anyway. Tell me the truth, no matter how much you think it may hurt me."

Dee was leaning against the doorjamb, her head down, her arms crossed tightly over her chest. "What good will that do?"

"What good's the silence done? What good have your threats to leave me done?"

"'Threats to leave me'!" Dee mimicked nastily. "As if you cared."

"I do care. And you know it. I feel abandoned, Dee."

"*You* feel abandoned!" Dee cried. "*You* do? What about me? Did you even think about me? You couldn't even let me finish high school before—" She stopped herself.

"Yes, I did think about you. Both your father and I did, if that's what you mean. Alice and I did, too."

Dee just stared. "I can*not* believe you, Mother," she said. "I simply cannot believe you."

Her mother nodded. "I know. Will you tell me what you're so angry at?"

Dee dropped her head and didn't respond for a while, and then she looked up at her mother and spit out, "Okay. I'll tell you what you want to know, then. I hate this filthy thing you have going with Alice, whatever it is. I hate her living here and Dad being in California. And I hate it that you're not even ashamed of what you're doing."

Dee's mother, who was an easy crier, was dry-eyed. She took a deep breath and then let it out again. "'This filthy thing,'" she mused. "'Whatever it is.' I'm sorry

you feel the way you do, as I told you, but I understand it. I really do."

Dee made a sound of disgust.

"And at least you're honest with me about what
you think. Nobody at the hospital was, really. *Their*
line was that what they called Alice's and my 'attach-
ment' to each other interfered with our efficiency. Of
course, they never put that on record in any way."

"Well, maybe you *did* interfere with each other's
efficiency. Did you ever think of that? Couldn't you
have just . . . pretended not to know each other at
work?"

For a time her mother did not respond. And then
she said, very calmly but with firmness too, "Yes, we
considered that. But we concluded the price of doing
it would have been too high."

"What's that?" Dee sneered. "Some kind of gay
pride thing?"

"I don't think in terms like that. I don't think anyone else should either."

"But you are gay, aren't you? Or bi, or something?"

"No. I'm not gay or bi or something. I simply refuse
to talk, or to think, in categories like the hateful ones
the world uses. I am what I am, Dee. I'm me. I'm not
some category any more than you are, and I'm no
more ashamed of loving Alice than I am of having
loved your father—or than I am of loving you."

"But you love her more than me and Dad. She

means more to you than we do. Otherwise, you'd just throw her out."

"That's not true. She's my *friend*, Dee, and I love her, just as you are my daughter and I love you. I would no more 'throw her out,' as you put it, just because you asked me to than I would do such a thing to you for her."

"So much for blood being thicker than water," Dee said acidly.

"You know, I never understood that saying—I guess because I never heard it used as other than an excuse for betrayal."

It was a remark that got Dee's full attention. She could still remember squinting through her burning, swollen eyes and thinking, for all her hurt and rage and fear, consciously thinking for the first time in her life, that maybe there was more to her mother than she'd acknowledged.

Within two weeks of Dee's move to Megan's, her mother had sold their home along with most of what was in it (Dee had refused to take anything) and, with Alice, had bought the farm near Wolfdale. Dee hadn't accepted any of their many invitations to visit, and she'd spent Thanksgiving and Christmas breaks with Megan and her family. But she continued to speak with her mother (and father) on the telephone, at least now and then. They wrote letters. They were still in one another's lives.

• • •

Dee had no difficulty recognizing the old stone farmhouse just outside Wolfdale from the many photographs her mother had sent of the renovations she and Alice had taken on. They'd done a lot of the work themselves: large portions of the carpentry, the rewiring, the painting, the laying of tile and carpet, and, of course, the landscaping. The place was by no means finished, but it was beginning to look like a home. Dee pulled through the gate in the high wrought-iron fence, built to shut out hungry nibbling deer, and parked behind her mother's ancient Honda. No sooner had she stepped from the car than she heard a squeal of delight, and her mother was suddenly taking her into her arms. "How are you, dear!" she cried, holding Dee a shade closer and longer than she was comfortable with. Her mother's slim body was as firm as a young boy's, and her dark blond hair, done as always in a single thick braid, smelled of apples and nutmeg. Dee avoided looking into her eyes, which she knew would be filled with tears.

"Now, I know you hate it when I cry," Dee's mother said, holding her at arm's length, "so I promise this is the last time I'm going to." Then she caught Dee close again. "Oh, Dee," her mother said into her neck. "It's so good to see you."

"Me too, Mom," Dee said. "Are you making applesauce?"

"No," her mother said, drawing away and laughing self-consciously, "but apples are in it. It's a Scandinavian fruit soup, actually, a cold soup. You boil up a lot of dried fruits with spices and make a puree."

Dee knew without asking that the fruits had been preserved by her mother and Alice.

"Sounds like one of Alice's recipes."

She'd meant the remark neutrally, but it brought her mother's head up. "Yes," she said. "I hope you like it. It'll be just the two of us for dinner, by the way— well, for the whole weekend, really. Alice has gone to Wisconsin to be with her family for Easter."

Dee smiled. So Alice had been able to go after all. She'd just gotten a new job working in a doctor's office in town and had wondered whether it was wise to ask for Easter weekend off. Even though Dee had made up her mind to be cordial, she was happy not to have to deal with Alice at all.

The hills in the distance were a hazy lime green in the late afternoon sunshine, and the air was pungent with the smell of compost and freshly turned earth. In the last two weeks, spring had taken hold of western Pennsylvania. Dee stretched, reaching up with both hands.

"Is your garden in?" she asked. "I'll bet the herbs are anyway."

"Come see," her mother said, her face luminous as she moved lightly across the front lawn. She always seemed to float everywhere, reminding Dee of a moth. "And I want to show you some things that weren't in any of the photos I sent."

The ample backyard ran out in a fenced-in rectangle divided in two. Beyond it were woods on all sides. The half of the rectangle farthest from the house was an orchard with a lot of new trees just starting to leaf out. The closer half was mostly garden, but by one side fence were a chicken coop, a new wooden shed with a fenced-in running yard, and in front of that, chained to stakes, two thoughtful-looking goats.

"You got your goats finally."

"And a dozen chickens. The goats are nannies. We got them from a man down the road to make milk and cheese. They'll be ready to breed next winter."

"Are they friendly?"

Dee's mother pulled a few young lettuce leaves from the garden and some sprigs of old parsley and handed them to her. "Go see what you think."

The goats got to their feet as Dee approached, the slitted pupils of their eyes making them seem both mild and demonic at the same time. They took the plants she offered delicately with their rubbery lips and chewed. When she scratched their bony heads, they butted gently at her hands, and then at her legs, for more.

Dee came back to her mother in the garden and looked around her. "Some of your herbs are up enough for me to see how many I remember."

"Just moved them out from the cold frames this past week. I don't know whether I told you, but I've got outlets for all the organic things I can raise."

Dee's mother then led her through the neatly laid-out beds that reminded Dee of those in the backyard of the Pittsburgh house. Herbs had always been a part of her life. Her mother had braided thyme and rosemary in her hair when she was young, and she could remember still the sharp aromatic bite of the gray sage that her mother burned in the kitchen to clear the air of negative energy. There had been long braided strands of sweet grass on the wall over her bed and over her parents' bed too. She remembered also her mother making herb vinegars of borage with its pink buds and vivid blue star-shaped flowers, of chive blossoms, of garlic and mint with lemon peel. And above all, she remembered the bunches of herbs drying in their unfinished attic, hanging from the long narrow laths like dead weeds until you touched them and they burst into giddy aromatic life.

"Do you remember this?" Dee's mother asked, squatting by a sprawling small-leaved plant. "You used to say its leaves were like little pine needles."

"Rosemary?"

"Close. Rosemary has pine needle leaves too. Here—" She broke off a sprig, crushed it in her fingers, and held it for her daughter to smell.

"It isn't thyme, is it?"

"Close again. Thyme's got the narrowest leaves of all. It's tarragon."

But Dee remembered fennel right away, and dill, of course, and sage, and garlic, and—with the help of a tiny new leaf to smell—basil.

"Basil. Oh, my," Dee said. "I haven't had pesto in more than a year."

"We're having it tonight, Dee-Dee—not from these plants, of course. I pureed and froze a lot of basil last summer. We had plenty, even if I didn't plant till July; it comes up like Jack's beanstalk. Do you remember the time you ate a whole plastic container full of it? Of pesto, I mean. You ate with one finger, scoop after scoop."

Dee laughed. "I got sick, I think, didn't I? Why didn't you stop me?"

"Pooh," her mother said. "Sick on basil, pine nuts, olive oil, garlic, and grated Parmesan cheese? That night, though, when you were sleeping, your whole room filled with the smell of garlic. Want to see the orchard, such as it is so far? And then I'll show you the chickens."

After they toured the property, Dee's mother pointed at an unspaded section of the garden. "I have about an hour's work left here. Why don't you take your bag upstairs—your bedroom's the middle one. We'll have some iced tea together when I'm finished."

"I'll help you," Dee said.

"No. I'd rather work alone, if you don't mind. Give me an hour."

It was not a rebuff, Dee knew. All the things her mother really cared about she preferred to do by herself. Still, Dee would have liked it that day if they'd stayed together.

Later, they sat on the back porch steps sipping some kind of subtly flavored iced tea, watching the world slip into twilight, the sky turning rose at first and then scarlet. Dee's mother got up and looked at the rim of the dying sun. "Such a terrible day Good Friday is, isn't it? A terrible, terrible day. That sky looks full of blood to me."

"You have to think of Easter," Dee said.

Dee's mother kept looking at the sky. "I suppose," she said in a dreamy voice. "But Easter never seemed real to me. Good Friday was what was real."

For dinner there was pesto as promised, freshly baked bread, the cold fruit soup, and some kind of stew in which there were whole chantarelles, the wild mushrooms with the scent of apricots that she had once hunted with her mother in the woods around Highland Park. And there were candles, of course, many, many candles, no two of them alike. Several mobiles made of prisms hung glittering over the sideboard, one of the few pieces of furniture Dee's mother had brought with her from their house in Pittsburgh. It gave Dee a creepy feeling to see it, as though she were looking at something stolen.

"I do love that drawing of you," Dee's mother said when they'd finished eating. She was smiling up at the copy of *Woman in the Window* hanging on the wall behind where Dee was sitting. Dee had noticed it earlier, of course, but was uncomfortable looking at her own nakedness with her mother.

"I want to show you something else," Dee said, getting up from the table.

When she came back downstairs with the rolled-up copy of Cory's drawing of Kate, she had her mother close her eyes. Then she took down the framed copy of *Woman in the Window* and taped Cory's new drawing up where it had been.

"Well," Dee said, "the light's not so good, but you can open your eyes now. This is a drawing of Kate Soffel. Cory sent it down with me as a present for you. What do you think?"

There was no need for Dee to explain who Kate Soffel was. She'd been living with her mother the whole time she was writing her paper. She'd also sent her a copy of Harry's film and had told her of their meeting in February and their working together on another piece of Kate's story.

Dee's mother looked at Cory's drawing for so long and with such intensity that Dee became uneasy.

"It's stunning. It's a little scary to me, but it's really stunning."

"What's scary? What do you mean?"

Dee's mother dropped her eyes. "Dee, I don't want you to get angry with me."

"I won't. Tell me what you see, Mom."

Dee's mother kept looking down for a moment, then nodded and got up from the table. "I'll try." She walked over to stand closer to Cory's drawing and looked at it from a couple of different angles.

"*It* isn't scary. It's . . . it's your involvement with someone with Cory's kind of talent that scares me."

Dee just stared at her mother.

Her mother looked back up at the drawing and gestured at it. "He's got a vision, you see—or maybe his vision has him. Anyway, you can see it in just the way he signs his name. It's runic somehow, mystical."

Cory's signature, if that's what it was, had always struck Dee too. He'd worked the initials of his name into a kind of monogram that reminded Dee of something stamped in metal. But runic? Mystical?

Her mother continued, "People who . . . have their own compasses for going where they're going, the way I think Cory does, are . . ." She didn't finish.

"Are not always easy to be around. You're right, Mom. Cory isn't. We have a lot we're working on." She hugged her mother quickly around the shoulders. "But I'm glad you can feel his talent. I'm awfully proud of him."

On both Saturday and Sunday, Dee slept deeply, dreamlessly, and late, and for the rest of the weekend she and her mother did just ordinary things. They walked. Dee watched her mother feed the goats and chickens. She sat at the kitchen table chattering on about school, gossiping while her mother cooked. She was more relaxed than she would have believed she could be.

But on the way back to Pittsburgh late Easter night, the more Dee thought of her mother's new life, of her father in California, of the uncertainty of things with Cory, the more uneasy she became as to where her place was. She was neither going home nor leaving it. Her home could be wherever she chose to make one. But where exactly was that to be?

CHAPTER 13

Megan was asleep by the time Dee got back to Pittsburgh, but she'd left one of her cartoons propped up on Dee's desk blotter:

The reverse side read:

PLEASE
DON'T
TALK TO HER
UNTIL AFTER WE
TALK, OK??
(WAKE ME UP
IF YOU NEED TO!)

Wake me if you need to? Something was up. Megan hated being awakened.

There were three pieces of mail for Dee under the cartoon. One was a note from Jury thanking her and Megan and Cory for their friendship, patience, and goodwill, "albeit in a failed endeavor." The second was a letter from the station manager of WHGH offering her an internship for the coming summer to work with Harriet Bromfield. The third envelope Dee just stared down at for several moments without opening. It was the one she'd addressed to herself and sent to the Division of Vital Records in New Castle. And then she did open it. Inside was a death certificate for Catherine Miller.

The single folded-up page was stamped with a red filing number and embossed with the seal of the Commonwealth of Pennsylvania. It was a photocopy of a filled-in official form, but the reproduction was of such wretched quality that Dee could barely read some of the entries, particularly at the bottom of the page. Tempted as she was to skim the document for the burial particulars, Dee sat down at her desk, tipped up the shade of her lamp to get as much light on the page as possible, and made herself go through the two columns of information item by item.

Kate was described as a divorced white female, aged forty-two. Her occupation was listed as that of dressmaker. She'd been born on July 26, 1867, of C. H. Dietrich and Maria Hauptmann Dietrich, themselves born in Germany. The second column contained first the medical particulars. A Dr. Stockler, or perhaps Stackler, certified that Kate had become ill with typhoid fever on or about August 16, that she had entered West Penn Hospital on August 22, and that he had treated her there until she died on August 30, 1909, at 10 A.M. Then came the name of Kate's undertaker, which Dee already knew: Lutz and Beinhauer, the firm whose records had been destroyed in a fire. Underneath that name, however, something else was written in a spiderish hand that was all but illegible: "Terminated at H. Tompson," it looked like. Or maybe the name was "Lawson." And following the name there was a date: "9/1/09."

Dee took the shade off her desk lamp and held the certificate almost next to the naked bulb.

Then, with a prickling of her scalp, she realized she'd read the final entry incorrectly.

The word wasn't "Terminated," it was "Cremated"! On September 1, 1909, two days after Kate had died, her body was cremated by someone or some agency named H. Tompson or H. Lawson!

Did H. Tompson or H. Lawson still exist today in some form, the way the undertaking firm of Lutz and Beinhauer did?

There was no Tompson or Lawson in the Yellow Pages under the heading of "Cremation," but there was the name H. Sampson, and in a box at the bottom of the page, the same firm was advertised as "Now in its third century of business." The office of the funeral parlor, Dee noticed, was on Neville Street in Oakland, right near Pitt.

Perhaps she should call Harry now and tell her what she'd learned. But it was nearly 2:00 in the morning, and Megan would not have insisted Dee talk with her first without reason. Also, if Dee could get what she hoped she was going to get from Sampson's tomorrow, wouldn't she then look even more professionally impressive to Harry than she would with just the death certificate?

She decided to leave a message with Harry's voice mail at the station, keeping things very general but doing what she could to whet Harry's appetite. She began by saying that the letter appointing her as summer intern had arrived from WHGH when she was down visiting her mother, and she thanked Harry again for getting her the job. Then she said she'd just received some information that was very important to the story they were after. "By tomorrow night," Dee concluded, "that is, by Monday night, April thirteenth, I may even have the *whole* story regarding a certain matter, if I catch a break or two. I hope your trip went well. I'm all caught up with school, by the way. And it will be *great* to see you again."

Dee was too excited to really sleep. For the rest of the night she just dozed, and Kate's image kept floating into her head. Kate had suffered with typhoid fever for fourteen days, the death certificate said, half of that time unhospitalized, which probably meant untreated. Dee had read about the disease. It was like having the flu at first, but then things got worse. You dehydrated. You couldn't keep anything down. You had terrible headaches and abdominal cramps. Alternately, you burned up with fever and shook with chills. But what killed you finally were the hemorrhages, storming the lungs in one seizure after another.

In her mind's eye, Dee kept seeing the figure of a thin, dark-haired woman lying in a white iron hospital bed, silent, eyes hollow, her white nightgown soaked with blood. No one, not a single visitor, not even a member of her family, the newspapers smugly reported, had come to West Penn Hospital to ease Kate's passing. From Harry and Jury, though, Dee knew that Kate's half sister Ellen—Jury's grandmother—had been there every day disguised as a nurse, because her husband, for the shame of it, had forbidden his wife to show herself publicly as Kate's sister. Dee imagined her coming in secret, bathing Kate's face and arms, and brushing out her thick dark hair, Kate whispering all the while, eyes wide and burning. Please, Ellie, please. Promise me, Ellie. Promise me.

Toward dawn Dee had a ghastly dream. She was in Paris at the time of the French Revolution. It was night, and she was part of a mob howling its way down a cobbled street behind a cart carrying a chained prisoner, a woman dressed in white shining armor, with long dark hair in a single braid like the one her mother wore. She was kneeling on a pile of straw, her hands clasped in prayer. At a kind of village square the mob spread out, yelling, thrusting torches into the air, gathering around a great pile of firewood heaped up in bundles at the foot of a blackened cross. Courteously, the woman was assisted from the rear of the cart, at which point Dee realized that she was not dressed in armor, but plated in segments like a beetle, and from the waist down her body was that of a goat. "Time for the milking, Dee," the woman called over to her in a kind of chant. "Time for the milking." And then somehow the woman was on the cross, nailed up at her wrists and feet. As flames licked around her and the mob screamed in triumph, the woman looked down at Dee, at Dee only, and smiled. And then she winked.

Dee got up and showered after that. She stuffed some casual clothes into a tote bag and put a notebook and some of the information about Kate into the attaché case Harry had given her. Then she dressed in the same skirt she'd worn when she'd first met Harry and went into the living room to wait for Megan to wake up.

After a time, Dee heard Megan's alarm. When she came out of the bathroom, Dee called out. "Once you're awake, let's talk."

Megan came in yawning with a cup of coffee and sat down on the chair opposite the couch. "How come you're all dressed up?" she asked. "Your visit to your mom's go okay?"

"It went okay. Could we talk about that later? Tell me about Harry, please."

"Oh, right," Megan said, snapping awake. "You didn't call her, did you?"

"Of course not. Not after your note."

Megan took a deep gulp of coffee and then, without looking at Dee, asked, "Why didn't you tell me you'd sent away for Kate's death certificate? And you didn't tell Cory either. And I'll bet you didn't tell Jury."

Dee felt her cheeks redden, and she shifted uncomfortably. "How do you know I sent for a death certificate?"

"Come on, Dee. I brought in the mail, okay? What else would be in a letter addressed to you in your handwriting from the Division of Vital Records in New Castle, Death Certificate Division, or whatever it was? Why didn't you tell me?"

Dee shifted her position again. "I didn't want the grief, I guess."

For a time Megan didn't answer. "Well," she said finally, "I guess I'd have given you some. Did you know you can be fined five thousand dollars *and*— not *or*—and be sent to prison for up to two years for lying to the state the way you did?"

Dee looked off. Then she made a face and said, "Sent to prison. Come on, Megs. I didn't rob a bank."

Megan came forward in her chair. "To tell the state in a signed statement that Kate is a relative of yours— your grandmother or something—which is what you'd have had to do to get a death certificate, is a crime, a second-class misdemeanor. I checked with my dad on this, Dee—and, no, I didn't tell him you were the one I was asking about. It's a form of perjury, 'falsely swearing to authorities' it's called, a violation of Statute 4904, which I looked up myself, and you better believe you can go to jail for it."

The two just stared at each other for a moment.

"Though I admit," Megan said, leaning back, "that

going to jail isn't really a possibility. You're right. It isn't a very big crime you've committed, and chances are the state wouldn't bother about it even if they knew what you'd done—unless somebody pushed them to press charges. Then they'd have to. And when they found you guilty—and they would; you've broken the law—it would be for a crime that's in a class known as 'violation of public trust.' It's only a misdemeanor, of course, not a felony. You'd get probation. But a crime in violation of the public trust is *not* something somebody looking for a job as a journalist would want on her record. You get me here, Dee?"

"This somebody who might push the state to prosecute me," Dee said after a time, "you think it's Harry, don't you?"

"It was the Spider Lady's idea that you send away for the death certificate, wasn't it?"

Dee smiled and shook her head. "As a matter of fact, it wasn't. Harry had nothing to do with it. In fact, she was the one who warned me *not* to write the state."

"She did, huh? Then how come she called *me* early Friday night, right after she got back into town, to ask whether you'd got a letter from the Division of Vital Statistics while she was gone?"

Dee didn't speak.

After a time, Megan asked, "Are you sure you didn't call her last night?"

"Of course I'm sure," Dee said crossly. And then

she added, "Well, I called her machine, but I didn't talk to *her.*" She told Megan the message she'd left at the TV station.

Megan nodded. "Okay. Nothing about the death certificate *specifically* then. That's good. See—this is what I wanted to tell you before you called her— Harry actually called *twice* on Friday. She called a second time about ten-thirty—woke me up too—to ask me to be sure to let her know right away if a letter from the Division of Vital Statistics came for you in the Saturday mail, because what was in it had to do with some research she wanted to get a head start with. She'd drive right over here, she said, to pick up such a letter. Does that sound at all funny to you?"

Again, Dee didn't say anything.

"Right. It did to me too. It sounded like some kind of double cross, frankly. So when those letters for you from WHGH and the state came on Saturday, I just sat on them."

Dee chewed the side of her lower lip, thinking. "Harry and I did have a conversation about how to get a death certificate just before she left for California." She told Megan about their conversation in the car. "I suppose," she finished by saying, "that Harry must have worked out that I wasn't going to be patient enough to wait for the station's lawyer to help us. She was right, of course."

Megan snorted a laugh. "What she worked out was a way of getting you to rake her chestnuts out of the fire for her."

Dee felt dazed. "I don't see that at all," she said. "Not at all. But even if it's true, where's the harm?"

"Dee-Dee," Megan sighed in exasperation. "You can be a real jerk sometimes, you know that? The harm is, she's got an edge on you now. She's got something she can use to pressure you if she needs to. *You're* the one who wrote the state and signed your name to a bunch of false statements. It's *your* check or money order they have on record. Harry's not involved at all."

"But what would Harry want to pressure me about?"

Megan simply looked at her in mock surprise. "Stop it, Dee, will you? You're not stupid."

For a moment Dee felt close to crumbling. She dropped her face into her hands and stayed that way for a time. Then she sat up again, shaking her head firmly.

"I'm sorry, Megs, but I just don't buy that Harry's out to betray me. You know the letter you put on my desk from WHGH? It was from the station manager, offering me an internship for this summer. Harry got me that. She gave me this attaché case. She's the one who told me I had to start taking college seriously, and that's why I'm caught up on all my schoolwork. She—"

"Oh, Dee," Megan interrupted. "You're not going to go through what a peach Harry is again, are you? How

171

she's going to help you win a Pulitzer and make Cory a star and all that?"

Dee felt her face redden again. "All I want to say is that I don't think I'm just a jerk for trusting Harry."

Megan didn't respond, and for a time they sat in silence. "Well," Megan said finally, "I better get going." She clapped both hands down on her knees and then got to her feet. "You did get the death certificate at least, yes? You know where Kate's buried?"

"Oh," Dee said, "I'm sorry. I should have told you. I don't know where she's buried *yet*, but we're not at a dead end anymore either." She took the certificate out of the notebook in her attaché case and showed Megan what she'd learned from it.

"So that's why you look like you've got an interview with IBM. You're going over to Sampson's this morning. You're not going to class."

Dee shook her head. "No, I'm not going to class. And, yes, I am going to Sampson's—if you'll lend me the car again."

Megan looked pointedly at the attaché case and tote bag.

"It's just sneakers and jeans. If Sampson's can tell me what I hope they can, I'm going to be standing beside Kate's ashes before the day's over. And I'll be able to tell you about it at dinner."

"Better take an umbrella or a jacket," Megan suggested. "There's supposed to be a thunderstorm this afternoon. And you'll have to give me a ride to Pitt; I'll be late otherwise."

On the way to drop Megan off, Dee raised the question that had been at the back of her mind ever since hearing about Harry's phone calls.

"Why was it so important to Harry to get the death certificate before I did, though? That one I can't figure out."

Megan looked over at her. "Harry's not going to take any chances with your knowing something she doesn't."

Dee didn't say anything else until they stopped at the traffic light by Pitt's Cathedral of Learning, where Megan got out and Dee slid behind the wheel. "You don't know any of that for sure about her, though, Megs. You just don't like her."

"Right," Megan said, nodding. "I don't." She started across the street but stopped and looked back from the crosswalk. "If you find the grave," she yelled, "are you going to . . . ?" But the end of what she said was lost in the sound of traffic as the light changed, and Megan had to run the rest of the way across Forbes Avenue.

CHAPTER 14

The firm of H. Sampson, Incorporated, had obviously been around for a while and looked to Dee as though it thought it had the right to be. It was made up of two stately brick houses, built originally as separate homes in Pittsburgh's mansion days, but joined now, as though in marriage, by a sort of corridor. Everything had been painted white.

Dee parked at the top of a sweeping circular driveway just to one side of a flagstone walk leading to the middle of the corridor. The office of H. Sampson, Incorporated, obviously. She checked her hair and makeup in the mirror, made sure her notebook was in her attaché case, and after reminding herself she had high heels on, got out of the car, breathing deeply a couple of times to still her nervousness. She was going to need some luck, of course, but a lot would depend on how she handled herself.

Just inside a set of double doors was a large reception area that felt like an expensively done living room. There was even a grand piano in a far corner. Sitting at a desk to the right was a woman who looked about fifty, wearing a suit, a very good one. She had a sweet, faintly plump face, a warm engaging smile, and she smelled like a sachet. "Karen Navers," a little plaque on her desk read. Dee would not have been surprised to hear her speak with a Southern accent, but she didn't. "May I help you?" she asked pleasantly.

Dee introduced herself as Dee Bromwell and, with a look of concern that she didn't have to feign, began reciting the script she had worked out the night before.

"I hope you can help me, Ms. Navers. I'm here on behalf of my family, really—they're all back in Philadelphia—to get some information about a relative of ours. She's my great-great-grandmother, and we're trying to find out where she's buried. She died out here in Pittsburgh in 1909."

"Won't you be seated, please?" Ms. Navers said gesturing. "I assume you've checked the obituaries."

"Oh, yes," Dee said, sitting down in a conveniently placed chair, "but there's nothing about where she was buried. There's no church record either."

"And we handled her funeral?"

"Well," Dee said, shifting her weight slightly, "you did and you didn't. That is, Sampson's did and didn't. Her undertaker was Lutz and Beinhauer. But evidently they had Sampson's cremate her body. So what I'm hoping, what our whole family is hoping, is that you'll know where her ashes are. Beinhauer's records were all destroyed."

"Yes," Ms. Navers said. "In a fire. Everything up to 1952. Are you sure your relative was cremated?"

"Yes," Dee said, opening her attaché case and getting the death certificate out of her notebook. "Let me show you."

"I ask only because cremation wasn't used much in the early part of the century, you know."

"It wasn't?"

"No," Ms. Navers said, taking the death certificate from Dee. "There was a lot of prejudice against the practice for religious reasons mostly. The Catholic Church forbade it, though it doesn't now. In fact, at the beginning of this century there were only two crematoriums east of the Mississippi. Sampson's was one."

"My goodness," Dee said with a tone of what she hoped was sophisticated surprise. "I never realized. The form isn't very legible, as you can see, but doesn't it say at the bottom there that Sampson's cremated the body?"

Ms. Navers nodded, absorbed in the document. "It certainly does, but I wonder—oh." She cut herself off, looked quickly at Dee, and then looked down again.

Dee felt a stab of fear. "What? What do you wonder?"

Ms. Navers colored slightly and didn't answer

right away. "Well," she said, "as you must have seen, your . . . great-grandmother, was she?"

"My great-*great*-grandmother."

"Was divorced. That may have been the reason for the cremation, you see. Women were deeply ashamed of divorce then. In most instances anyway."

Dee didn't say anything.

"I was wondering, in other words," Ms. Navers said in prim self-reproach, "about things that are none of my business to wonder about. I'm sorry."

"It's okay, Ms. Navers. Everybody in the family's wondered about why she was divorced too. None of us know very much about this lady. Do you think you'd have any record of . . . ?" Dee let the sentence trail.

"Of course," Ms. Navers said, getting to her feet. She wrote down a couple of things from the death certificate on a small pad. "Please sit down," she smiled. "This shouldn't take me long."

"My family will really appreciate this, Ms. Navers," Dee said, sitting on the edge of her upholstered chairs.

Ms. Navers turned, walked down the hall of the corridor that stretched out behind her, and then vanished through a door on her left. Dee got to her feet again and began to pace the room, moving carefully around the antique furniture, looking at the watercolors hanging on the walls without really seeing any of them. She jounced up and down on the carpet slightly; it was as springy as moss.

After a while a door opened and closed, and there was Ms. Navers in the corridor carrying a large gray ledger that she held with both hands at an awkward angle out from her body. "These things are filthy with dust," she said as she lay the ledger on her desk blotter and sat down behind it. She wiped her hands with a Kleenex, checked the front of her suit, and then picked up the death certificate still lying on the desk. "Now," she said, "this relative of yours. Catherine Miller. She had two other names as well, did you know?"

Dee didn't see any way around having to reveal at least part of what she knew. She sat down again and picked up her notebook from the desk. "I think I have something written down about that here somewhere."

"Yes," Ms. Navers nodded. "Dietrich was her maiden name. She married someone named Soffel."

Someone named Soffel? Apparently, Ms. Navers had no idea who Kate Soffel was.

"We handled her all right, but I'm afraid your family may be in for something of a shock." She then opened the ledger at a piece of paper marking the page, turned the book around, and pushed it to Dee's side of the desk.

The ledger page was a long printed form with spaces for entries such as "Washed and layed out by," "Attitudes by," "Number of carriages supplied for procession," and so on. Most had been left blank. At the top of the page, however, under "Name of deceased" was written "Catherine Miller (née Dietrich; m. Soffel)," and at about the middle of the page alongside "Interment at" was written "See special instructions from L. Beinhauer attached." A handwritten note dated August 31, 1909, had been attached to the page with a rusty paper clip:

According to the wishes of the deceased, and with the express permission of her family, we hereby submit the body of Catherine Miller to H. Sampson and Sons for cremation. The ashes are to be collected by Mrs. Henry Markwardt in order to be deposited in the grave of Miss Miller's mother. At the request of both the deceased and her family, none of this information is to be released to the public.

Lutz and Beinhauer, Licensed Morticians

Dee swallowed and read the note again. And then she read it once more still. Kate's ashes had been turned over to Jury's grandmother for her to place in Kate's *mother's* grave! And no one outside Kate's family was to know this!

No wonder people had never been able to find where Kate was buried.

"I'm sorry," Ms. Navers said after a time. "Your relative was in some kind of trouble, obviously. I hope this won't be a blow to you or to your family."

179

"I'm sorry," Dee said from the whirl of her own thoughts. "What did you say?"

Ms. Navers repeated herself. "Oh, no," Dee said. "It's all right. Thank you, but it's all right."

Ms. Navers looked down, shook her head several times very slowly, and then looked back up at Dee. "You know, Dee," she said gently, "you don't have to search very far in any family to find trouble—and there's always more than one side to things."

"Oh," Dee said, nodding. "I know. I know there is."

"At least you should have no trouble finding your relative's grave, though. That's something."

"Yes," Dee said distractedly. "Yes, of course." But then, realizing she should draw all she could from Ms. Navers's expertise, she asked, "I mean, what makes you say I should have no trouble?"

Ms. Navers smiled and picked up the death certificate. "Whatever name your great-great-grandmother lived under, *her* mother was . . ."—she found the place—"Maria Hauptmann Dietrich. I'm assuming she too died in Pittsburgh."

"She must have." Maria, Maria Louisa, was Kate's father's first wife, and they had lived together for years in the section of Pittsburgh known as Mount Washington. Why wouldn't she have died and been buried in the city?

"Do you happen to know the year?"

Dee couldn't recall it, but she had Harry's data

sheet in her notebook. "I'm sure I have it in my notes somewhere."

"Fine. But even if you don't, here's what you do." And Dee, doing her best to look enlightened, let Ms. Navers tell her a lot of things she already knew about how to research city records, the files of old newspapers, even how to get to Carnegie Library.

And then Dee asked the question she really wanted answered. "Kate's church down on Smithfield Street had no record of her being buried with her mother. Do you have any idea why?"

Ms. Navers smiled. "Kate. That's what you call her? That's nice. They have no record because they keep a record only of official burials. The rite of burial, you see, was—Here. Let me see the ledger again, please. I want to be sure that I saw what I thought I saw."

Dee turned it around and slid it across the desk, and Ms. Navers read Lutz and Beinhauer's note again.

"Yes," she said. "It says here that the ashes were 'to be *deposited* in the grave of Miss Miller's mother.' That's not an official burial being alluded to, one for which there was a religious ceremony, and therefore it was not one the church would feel obligated to keep a record of."

"You mean Kate's sister might have just gone out to where their mother was buried and . . . poured Kate's ashes on the ground?"

Ms. Navers smiled. "That's *possible,* of course, but usually people had—" She stopped herself and then started again. "That wouldn't have been considered *respectful,* you see. In fact, there probably was some sort of ceremony—an 'inurnment' was what they called it—but that was always arranged strictly with the cemetery, which sometimes kept records and sometimes didn't."

"What's an 'inurnment'?"

"It's the burial of the urn and the ashes both— rather like the way a body is buried in a coffin? I've even seen urns made in the shapes of coffins."

"Coffins! Really!"

"Oh, yes, indeed." She held her hands apart. "About a foot and a half long. Beautiful things, even though they were strictly for burying. Made of wood or polished bronze. People sealed things up inside them with the ashes, like photographs or old letters. Keepsakes. 'Urn' is a kind of metaphor, actually. I've seen them in the shapes of small mausoleums, with tiny stained-glass windows and the name of the family engraved on the door. I saw one urn that was in the form of a Greek temple, made of pure silver, which horrified Mr. Sampson, of course, the suggestion of paganism."

"Incredible," Dee said, shaking her head. "Incredible. And they dug a regular grave just for little . . . urns like that?"

"Oh, my goodness, no, particularly if they were buried in already occupied plots. To go six feet down in a tenanted grave could . . . could run you into problems, if you see what I mean. A foot down or so they'd be buried. They'd keep things to scale."

"My," Dee said, getting slowly to her feet. "There's a lot more to all of this than I thought there'd be." She shook hands with Ms. Navers, thanking her profusely. Then she picked up the death certificate and put it back in her notebook.

"There's one other thing I'd appreciate, Ms. Navers, if it's allowed. Do you think I could have a photocopy of that page of the ledger for my family? That page and the note too? I'll be glad to pay you."

"Oh, heavens," Ms. Navers said with a gesture of deprecation. "Of course, Dee. No need for payment." But she stayed sitting, staring down at the closed ledger in front of her.

"What's . . . the matter?" Dee asked.

Ms. Navers looked off and then gave a small self-conscious laugh. "I know you'll probably think me silly, but I'd like *you* to do something for *me* if you don't mind."

"Of course," Dee said. "Certainly."

"Dee, when you find where this woman's ashes are, where Kate's ashes are, will you see that she gets some flowers? Some fresh flowers to be left with her—and with her mother too?"

"Of course," Dee said. "I was planning to do that anyway." Then she remembered some of the graves at Smithfield Cemetery with flowers planted by them. "Better yet," she said, "maybe I'll get her some permanent flowers, if the cemetery allows it. Flowers I can plant."

Ms. Navers smiled, rose, and picked up the ledger from her desk. "I'll be just a minute," she said as she stepped down the corridor.

Waiting, Dee sat down again on the edge of her chair and checked her watch. It was only a little after 10:00, and she was no more than ten minutes from Carnegie Library. She had the final pieces to the puzzle of where Kate was buried; she was sure of it. But she was uneasy. She'd been careful. Ms. Navers didn't know who she'd been inquiring about. She hadn't even given her real name. Harry couldn't have handled things any better. Still . . .

Dee heard a door close, and Ms. Navers came in with some photocopied pages, which she gave Dee.

"Forget-me-nots might be nice," she said. "They're perennials, and you'll have no trouble getting them at the nursery now."

"I'll make a point of it, Ms. Navers," Dee said, shaking hands a second time. "And thank you again for all your help."

CHAPTER 15

I t wasn't until Dee was in the parking lot of the Carnegie Library that she noticed she'd come away with both the original note Lutz and Beinhauer had written Sampson's and the photocopy of it Ms. Navers had made for her. A mistake obviously; Dee would drop the original back at Sampson's first chance she got.

On her way into the library, however, it suddenly occurred to her that without Lutz and Beinhauer's note, no one else was ever going to be able to pick up the trail of Kate's ashes, whether they had a copy of her death certificate or not. What would a professional do in such a situation? Dee decided she'd better wait to talk over how to handle things with Harry.

Within twenty minutes, changed into her sneakers and jeans, Dee zipped out of the library's ladies' room crackling with purpose. Kate's mother, according to

Harry's data sheet, had died in 1881, when Kate was fourteen. The city records supplied the month and day, and not long after that, Dee was copying an obituary from the evening edition of the *Pittsburgh Gazette:*

> **Dietrich, Maria Louisa,** formerly of Mt. Washington, beloved wife of Conrad H. Dietrich, died March 7, 37 years, 6 mos., and 22 days. Funeral March 9, 10:00 A.M. First German Protestant Evangelical Church, Sixth and Smithfield. Interred Troy Hill Cemetery.

Interred *Troy Hill Cemetery*! Kate's mother had been buried in Troy Hill?—which meant, of course, that Kate was not in Smithfield Cemetery at all, no matter what her obituaries said.

Dee checked her watch. It was almost lunchtime. She had never been to the section of Pittsburgh known as Troy Hill, but one of the librarians in the microfilm room assured her that the community was no more than half an hour away by car and told her exactly how to get there. "Over the Highland Park Bridge, straight down Route Twenty-Eight, turn right on Rialto, and head for the clouds. It's the land that time forgot up there." The librarian smiled. "You'll see. And there's only one cemetery in town."

Dee wolfed down two nutrition bars in the car. After crossing the bridge and making the turn off the highway, she had no trouble seeing what the woman meant about heading for the clouds on Rialto Street. It was the steepest hill she'd ever driven; she had to scrunch herself down almost to the top of the steering wheel even to be able to see ahead of her. At the top of the hill the road leveled suddenly into a crossing of four or five streets. Without really thinking, Dee took the first turn to her left and almost immediately found herself in the middle of a kind of village square dominated by a stone firehouse with its doors open. At the corner of the building was a grotesquely carved, life-sized wooden statue of a fireman holding a small boy in his arms, both of them staring owlishly at nothing.

Less than five minutes later, directed by a live fireman, Dee was on Lowrie Street, cruising by the Troy Hill Cemetery on her right—actually, the Voegtly Evangelical Church Cemetery, according to a plaque on the wrought-iron fence that ran alongside it. It wasn't very big, no more than one-third the size of Smithfield. It ran for only a quarter of a mile or so along Lowrie Street and extended out for about the same distance to a great open space, the edge of a cliff, Dee suspected. The whole of downtown Pittsburgh would be visible from there, she imagined, the whole South Side too.

Dee drove almost to the end of the cemetery without seeing anything like an office anywhere. She made a U-turn and then turned again by the second of two open gates in the fence. Following the example of a number of other cars, she pulled about halfway up onto a brick sidewalk.

Then she got out to look around. On the other side of the street for as far up and down Lowrie as she could see was a line of row houses set on top of a slope at the ends of long flights of concrete steps. Dee had seen the same style of high narrow buildings in other Pittsburgh working-class communities. Most of the old frame structures had been remodeled with aluminum siding, but they still resembled bricks set on end.

The sun suddenly ducked behind a cloud, and Dee looked off to the line of scudding gray moving in from the southwest. The storm Megan had mentioned. While getting her windbreaker from the backseat, she noticed three middle-aged women, all with kerchiefs on their heads, watching her from the stoop of one of the row houses she'd passed. She waved, but none of them waved back. She pulled on her jacket, locked the car, and walked back to talk to them.

The women didn't warm a bit to Dee's story about trying to locate the grave of her great-great-grandmother. Their expressions reminded her of the wooden fireman's stare, and they answered her questions almost entirely with monosyllables. What little they did say was spoken with an accent of some sort, as though English were not their native language.

Did the women know, Dee asked, where she could find a record of who was buried where in the cemetery? No. Did they know whether Voegtly Evangelical

Church still existed somewhere? (Dee pronounced it "*Vote*-ly," to their scornful amusement; "Veckly," they corrected her.) No. Did the women know anyone who *would* have the information she needed? No. There was no cemetery office? There was not.

Dee thanked them for their time, went back across the street, and for a moment just stood looking through the fence at the irregular rows of tombstones, one of which she knew marked the grave of Maria Louisa Dietrich, where Kate Soffel's ashes were buried. But which one? Way off over the South Hills there was a low rumble of thunder. Small as the cemetery was, Dee knew she couldn't hope to search the whole of it by herself before it rained, but she figured she could at least scan a couple of rows by starting from the corner where the last house on Lowrie came up against the cemetery's side fence. From there she'd work her way down to the edge of the cliff and back again. Maybe she'd get lucky.

She took off, half running up to the cemetery's first open gate. In a few moments, she'd reached the cornermost stone, which recorded the death of a woman named Spitzhaben in 1874. The time frame was right for Maria anyway, who'd died in 1881, and the name sounded German.

"Who are you looking for now?" a voice boomed above Dee, almost making her leap out of her skin.

It was a woman sitting in an old-fashioned wooden

rocking chair on the elevated porch of the house beside the cemetery. She had on a heavy tan sweater and a scarf draped over her head and also wound around her neck. Her face was leathery looking and seamed with wrinkles. Alongside her, in a harness attached to a leash, crouched the largest cat Dee had ever seen.

"*Now?*" Dee exclaimed in answer to the woman's question. "I've never been here before."

The woman's eyes were small and black and glittered in her wrinkled skin like chips of dark glass. "I didn't *ask* you whether you've been here before," she roared. "I *know* you've never been here before, so I wouldn't *have* to ask you that, would I?" She pointed a finger at Dee. "*Would* I?"

The woman looked as though she too should speak with an accent, but her English was perfect. "I guess not," Dee said.

"Well then?" the woman thundered, staring at Dee impatiently. "*Well* then, I say?"

"Well then, *what*?" Dee asked, raising her own voice to match the woman's volume.

The woman cocked her head like a sparrow and stared at Dee. "You're not a very bright child, are you? I asked you who you're looking for."

Dee considered turning away but decided not to. Very deliberately and in a loud voice she announced: "I'm looking for the grave of my grandmother."

"There," the woman bellowed down to the cat,

jouncing it by its leash as if in triumph. "Didn't I say so? Isn't that precisely what I said?" The cat paid her no attention. "Name of?"

For a moment Dee just stared, thinking the woman was talking to the cat.

"Name!" the woman barked, making Dee start again. "What's the name?"

"Dietrich," Dee yelled back. "Maria Louisa Dietrich. Born 1844. Died 1881. Her obituary says she's here, but I don't know where."

The woman folded her hands in her lap, dropped her head, and closed her eyes.

My God, Dee thought, she's going to sleep. Like the dormouse in *Alice in Wonderland.* Dee shifted her weight from one foot to the other. Time was crucial to her, and here she was mixed up with what was obviously the local loony.

"Look," she cried up to the huddled figure, "can you please tell me where I can get a record of the people buried in here?"

The woman opened her eyes and glanced down at Dee scornfully. "You needn't shout, young woman," she said in a normal tone of voice. "I still hear perfectly. As for the record, *I* am the record. I know everybody in here. I'm simply getting all the Dietrichs in mind. But it's not your grandmother's grave you want to find, is it?"

"What?" Dee stammered. "What do you mean?"

"A woman born in 1844 would be your great-grandmother, surely, your great-grandmother *at least*. More likely, she was your great-great-grandmother?"

"Oh," Dee said with a nervous laugh. "Did I say 'grandmother'? My great-great-grandmother is what I meant to say."

"But you *didn't* say that, did you?" the woman responded tartly, getting to her feet. "You spoke as though two generations don't mean anything."

Dee bit her tongue. Let it go, she advised herself. Just stick to business.

The woman looped the loose end of the cat's leash over the porch railing and tied it. "Stay here," she said either to Dee or to the cat, and went into her house. The cat, which hadn't moved, watched Dee with eyes like yellow suns. Thirty pounds it must weigh, Dee thought. Maybe even more. How did the old lady stay alone in a room with that much cat?

In a few moments, the woman was back with a pair of gloves and a toy cane tucked under one arm. After undoing the cat's leash from the railing, she pulled on her gloves, and then she raised the cane over her head—except that the cane turned out to be a toy whip, like those sold at the circus. She cracked it smartly in the air, and the sound rang like a shot, jolting the cat to its feet, tail puffed, eyes the size of half-dollars.

"Now," the woman said as she marched down her porch steps and along the brick sidewalk of Lowrie

Street, "meet me down at the gate. There are three groupings of Dietrichs in Voegtly; no single graves." She and the cat went at such a pace that Dee, on her side of the fence, had to hurry to keep up with them. "We may have to visit all three to find Maria, you understand. I have only family names for those who were buried before the twentieth century—and their location, of course. All the others I know by their full names."

At the cemetery gate the woman pointed with her whip in the direction of the cliff edge, and Dee fell in beside her, careful to choose the side away from the cat.

In some ways, the cemetery reminded Dee of Smithfield. There were a lot of German names—Doerschner, Wenig, Kleinbaum—and a lot of the same kinds of carvings on the headstones, of wings and urns and drooping trees. But she noticed different carvings too, of skulls and crossbones, of shambling skeletons, and the area in general was nowhere near so well tended as Smithfield. There didn't seem to be a road or a sidewalk anywhere, and the ground was like that of a pasture, humped and irregular, difficult to walk, covered with weeds and field grass. A couple of grave sites were brightened by clumps of blooming crocuses—which made Dee think of the forget-me-nots she'd forgotten to buy—and occasionally there was a plastic vase or a small washed-out American flag. But there were only a few obelisks, no mausoleums, and lots of headstones that were leaning or had fallen and broken. Perhaps Voegtly Cemetery was a more fitting repository for Kate's ashes than a place of peace would have been, but Dee found it depressing. She wanted to ask the old woman whether living alongside it ever bothered her, but one look at the grim leathery face decided her not to. The woman had said she knew where all the Dietrichs were buried. No reason to risk offending her.

The cat stopped, nosing interestedly at a headstone.

"Not *there,*" the old woman said, tugging the cat toward an open section of ground. "You wouldn't like someone pissing on your grave, would you?"

The cat circled a bit and then went into a crouch. When it had finished, the woman took a small plastic bag from under her sweater, picked up what the cat had left, and put the sealed bag in her pocket. The cat extended its claws, stretched itself, and yawned, showing teeth like spikes.

"That's . . . quite a cat," Dee said as they continued walking. "It's the biggest cat I've ever seen."

The woman didn't say anything.

"Is it like . . . a pet?"

"Sometimes," the woman said.

"What's its name?"

"Harold, of course," the woman snapped crossly, popping her whip and stepping briskly forward. As if in answer, there was another low roll of thunder. The line of clouds over the South Hills had moved closer.

For a while the two walked in silence.

"What do you want with her anyway?" the old woman asked after a time.

"My . . . relative? I'd just like to know where she is, that's all. Pay my respects. I want to get some flowers to plant for her too."

"She died in 1881; that's over a hundred years ago. Nobody in your family ever checked to see where she was before this?"

Dee felt her stomach begin to knot. "There was a split in my family," she said carefully. "A divorce. I think I'm the only one who's ever come up here. In fact, I'm pretty sure I'm the only one who knows she's in Troy Hill."

The woman stopped walking and turned to look at Dee. "You might have brought some flowers with you," she said, but as though advising her, not in reproach.

"I thought," Dee said, looking her full in the eyes, "I thought that today we'd . . . we'd just get acquainted. I thought I'd bring the flowers the *next* time I come. Also, I didn't know whether the cemetery would let me plant them." And Dee swore to herself she would make it a point to come back with flowers. "I'm going to get some forget-me-nots and crocuses and maybe some of those white flowers"—she pointed—"that look like daisies."

"Grecian windflowers."

"Yes. Grecian windflowers."

"Will any of your family come up with you?"

"I doubt it. But that's okay. I'll come back alone."

The woman's small eyes were unblinking and unreadable. And then she looked down and smiled slightly. "'Get acquainted,'" she repeated. "I haven't heard that from very many people who come up here, and the people who *live* up here, like those three biddies you were talking to, think I'm crazy." She chuckled. "Of course, it is sort of crazy, isn't it, that we should think of the dead as . . . well, dead, but not dead too, as alive somewhere—and I don't mean in heaven or anything like that. We think of them as alive out *here* in some way, as people to get acquainted with, able to enjoy crocuses and the carnations some people bring out on Memorial Day. We know perfectly well that there's nothing down there but . . . compost." She chuckled again. "But we do it, don't we? Some of us do anyway."

"Do you really know the names of everyone in here?"

The woman smiled fully, splitting her face into even more wrinkles. "Yes, indeed, child. Yes, indeed. And I've been to every interment here for the past sixty years." She stopped, as though thinking about what she'd just said. "Sometimes," she added, "I'm the only one there."

She's like Eleanor Rigby in the old Beatles song, Dee thought, picking up rice in the place where the weddings have been. Except with her, it's funerals.

The woman pointed with her whip to a cluster of gravestones off to the left, quite close to the cliff edge at the back of the cemetery. "Those are Diet-richs," she said. "Go and see which ones. After you check them, I want to show you something."

Dee hurried ahead to the stones, a grouping of four set in irregular relation to one another, like people sitting around in a living room. The first stone she looked at was for a Karla Dietrich who'd died in 1885. All three of the others were for male Dietrichs who'd died later.

"Be sure to check at ground level for plaques," the woman called, coming up behind her.

Dee did. There weren't any. She looked back at the woman, made a face, and shook her head. Then she went to the edge of the cliff. Almost directly below she could see the Allegheny River, then not very far out in the water, a section of an island, then more river, and beyond that a crowd of factories and warehouses. To the far right was downtown Pittsburgh, laced gracefully with soaring thruways, its skyscrapers shining triumphant in the sun. To the left in the distance the South Hills had already disappeared behind the curtain of approaching rain.

"Now, remember," the woman said, approaching Dee, "we have two other places to check. We'll find your Maria."

Your Maria made Dee smile. "I really do appreciate your helping me this way," she said. "Thank you." She stopped. "I'm sorry, I don't know your name."

"Seltsham," the woman said. "Ella Seltsham. And

it's my own name too, not some man's. I've never been married. I was born in that house where you found me. Lived there all my life. Eighty-seven years."

Dee introduced herself as Diane Bromwell. Dee Bromwell. "If I hadn't met you, I don't know what I'd have done. The other people I ran into"—she glanced back over her shoulder at the cramped-looking houses facing the cemetery—"the ones you called the biddies, they didn't seem much interested in whether I found my great-great-grandmother or not."

"I'm probably harder on them than I ought to be," Ms. Seltsham said. "We all have our own lives to live, you know, our own troubles, and people up here have always had to work too hard just to stay alive to care much about . . . things like history. Beauty. Maybe that's why they've never paid much attention to the view."

"What do you mean?"

Ms. Seltsham pointed her whip in the direction from which they'd come. "Do any of those houses seem built to take in the view? They have those teeny-tiny windows because people had to conserve heat."

She was right. There were no picture windows in any of the houses, no balconies or verandas, and only the briefest of porches. The houses marched along the crest of the ridge like a row of pickets.

"But out *there*," Ms. Seltsham said, pointing with her whip to the view in the other direction, "is a piece of history worth caring about. In fact, there are all kinds of pieces of all kinds of histories out there if you know how to look for them—lots of them ugly, but not all, not all of them, by any means. See those buildings off to the right down there? That's just the beginning of the H. J. Heinz factory. A lot of people up here used to work for Heinz. Do you know he had all of his food-processing ladies given manicures once a week, and he had cork floors put in his stables just to save his horses' feet? And that island down there just in front of us: that's Herr's Island, where the stock-yards used to be. They'd bring the pigs and steers in on barges or by rail." She turned slightly to point to the left. "That's the main way they came, over that bridge, brought in by the Pennsylvania Railroad. And my, what a stench we lived in up here when the stock-yards were going strong, particularly in the summer. In fact, they used to raise a lot of pigs up here and drive them down Rialto Street—'Pig Alley' it was nick-named—to be slaughtered in the yards."

"Really!" Dee exclaimed. "They drove pigs down that steep hill?"

"Oh, yes, indeed," Ms. Seltsham replied, nodding vigorously. "Yes, indeed. I would hear them from my bedroom, always just at dawn, squealing and grunting, and the terrible sound of the sticks on their backs and the cursing men. I went screaming to Papa the first time they woke me, to get him to make it all stop, but he couldn't, of course; of course, he could not."

On and on Ms. Seltsham talked from their lookout, folding past and present into each other, connecting the visible with the invisible. She spoke of the Voegtly Evangelical Church, which at one time had owned the very cemetery in which they were standing. The church used to be down on the flats by the river, just catty-corner from the main building of the Heinz factory complex, but it had been swept away years ago in the first wave of the new highway program. And along this same ridge they were standing on, down toward Millvale, her father had shot forty-pound wild turkeys when she was a little girl, and the fat perch he'd hauled up from the Allegheny were as long as she was tall then. She talked of the inclines, all but two of them gone now, and the old cable cars, sixteen of which at one time rose from the shores of the Monongahela all the way up the face of Mount Washington. Another one had even come up here, up from the shores of the Allegheny River to Troy Hill. For a while it ran anyway. Its old track bed was buried now under the blacktop of Rialto Street.

But Dee was too anxious to locate the grave of Maria to listen properly. It was already 2:30 P.M., she saw, and she was nervous about the weather. She didn't like thunderstorms. "Think we'd better head back?" she asked, looking up. "Looks like a storm's coming."

CHAPTER 16

Ms. Seltsham glanced up at the clouds racing toward them. "We've got some time yet. Harold will let us know. I want to show you something." Cracking the whip, she turned and strode off, the cat trotting beside her as amiably as a trained pony.

About twenty yards back toward Lowrie Street, Ms. Seltsham stopped in the middle of an open section of ground and turned to Dee. "Come tell me what you see here."

Flat on the ground was a green metal marker surrounded by a number of blooming crocuses:

> **Matthew Quintel**
> **152nd Pa. Artillery**
> **Born 1850. Enlisted 1863.**
> **Discharged 1864. Died 1894.**

Dee read it and read it again, and then swallowed hard, not knowing what she was supposed to see.

"The dates, child," Ms. Seltsham said softly. "Look at the dates, child."

Dee did, and then she suddenly saw. Born 1850. Enlisted 1863. He'd been only thirteen. The boy had been a soldier at the age of thirteen. Could that be right?

"Yes," Ms. Seltsham said in the same soft voice. "A drummer boy most probably, but a soldier nevertheless, fighting with the Federal troops. He was wounded, I should think, discharged only a year after he enlisted—but not so badly that he didn't live thirty more years. It couldn't have been just a minor wound, though; if it had been, they'd have patched him up and sent him back. Maybe he lost an arm or a leg. At the Battle of Gettysburg? At Vicksburg? Both were fought in 1863. I've wondered a lot about young Matt Quintel and why he enlisted to begin with. Adventure? Trouble of some sort?" She looked up at Dee and smiled self-deprecatingly. "I've even tried to imagine what he looked like."

Dee nodded slowly, remembering the image she'd had of Kate lying in the hospital with her thick dark hair. "Oh, yes," she said. "I've done that too. There's no family of his around anywhere that could help you? Somebody planted those crocuses."

"I did. There's no family of his that ever comes here. That's why I planted them."

"Maybe the government has some records."

"I'm sure they do, but I wouldn't feel right poking around that way without the family's permission."

Dee didn't say anything.

Ms. Seltsham cleared her throat. "Maybe," she said offhandedly, "you'd like to have a cup of tea when we're finished."

"Of course," Dee said, touched. "Of course. Thank you."

A heavy roll of thunder made them both look up and raised a peculiar cry from the cat. He sat back on his haunches, muzzle pointed to the sky, and began to howl, long drawn-out howls, as though announcing something. The line of swirling black clouds from the south had almost reached the Allegheny River. A wind had risen.

"It's going to rain all right," Ms. Seltsham said, "but I saw you park your car up on Lowrie."

"Yes. Where's the next bunch of Dietrichs?"

"Up alongside that red stone obelisk. There are six, I think."

Dee took off at a dead run and looked quickly at all six headstones. Only three of the graves held women, and the only one of them with dates that even approximated Maria's was that of a Helga Dietrich, born 1849, died 1899.

"Nothing," Dee yelled back, cupping her hands, but Ms. Seltsham had her head down against the wind and Dee didn't know whether she'd heard her.

The sky had darkened. There was a quick blue-white flash followed almost immediately by an earsplitting crack of thunder. The cat tossed his head against the pull of the leash, digging in his feet and claws. Dee could hear him hiss and spit even over the wind. "*Stop it, Harold,*" she heard Ms. Seltsham roar, leaning back on the leash as though trying to control the thrashings of a giant kite. "Stop it, sir! The last graves . . ." But her voice was drowned by the wind.

"Where?" Dee screamed. "Where?" She ran partway back so she'd be able to hear.

"By the gateway. Not the one you went through. The one straight ahead there."

Without a word, Dee whirled and streaked the fifty yards or so up to the second gateway of the fence, which was only about twenty-five yards from her parked car. The first splats of rain hit her face.

On one side of the gateway were two matching gravestones, one for a Katrina Dietrich who'd died in 1900, the other for her husband, Helmut, who'd died five years later. Frantic, Dee checked the two gravestones closest to them. Roth. Bachman. Dee raced to the other side of the gateway. No Dietrichs there. Had all of her hard work come to nothing, then? She stood open to the storm in the middle of the gateway, sick at heart and furious. Ms. Seltsham lumbered up, bowed under the rain, her long skirt billowing out behind her. Over one shoulder was her cat leash, which she held at her chest with both hands, dragging Harold on his back. The cat wailed like a banshee.

"She's not here," Dee said in accusation. "She isn't in here."

Another brilliant flash came with another earsplitting crack, and there was a smell of cheese. The cat leaped straight into the air, eyes starting from their sockets, tail the size of a feather duster. Even in the middle of that roaring world, the cat's yowl pushed Dee back a step.

"Let's head for your car, Dee. This is dangerous."

Burst after burst of lightning flickered around them as the rain drove down in great sheets.

It wasn't until they were alongside the car that Dee thought about having to share it with Harold. She'd sooner have been locked up with a Bengal tiger.

"Wait!" Ms. Seltsham screamed from the passenger side as Dee seemed about to get into the driver's seat. After looping and knotting the leash around the mirror on the passenger side, Ms. Seltsham waddled around to Dee. "Let me in first," she bellowed over the wind and rain, and then she added something unintelligible about the cat.

In a moment, from inside the car, the two women just sat streaming water, watching Harold scrabbling at the side window, ears plastered down against his head, his face fierce with outrage. "He has to be able to see me," Ms. Seltsham explained. "He'll go under the car eventually." Eventually he did, continuing to voice his displeasure.

"You must have missed a Dietrich somewhere," Dee said sullenly.

"Impossible," Ms. Seltsham said with a quick shake of her head. "Absolutely impossible. If she'd been buried here by a church in 1881, there would have been a headstone. They didn't allow people in this cemetery without one. And if there were a headstone here with the name of Maria Louisa Dietrich on it, I'd know where it was."

The rain on the car roof was like a continuous roll of drums. The windshield had turned into a waterfall.

"Do you happen to have Maria's obituary with you?" Ms. Seltsham asked Dee after a time. Her tone was cool. "I need to see the exact wording." She took a pair of reading glasses out from under her sweater. Without speaking, Dee got her notebook out of her attaché case in the backseat and handed Ms. Seltsham what she'd copied from the *Gazette*. For a moment the older woman just read. Then she smiled and nodded. She took off her reading glasses and looked at Dee. "My dear," she said, "I'm afraid it's you who has missed something. Your great-great-grandmother was never *in* this cemetery. This is *Voegtly* Cemetery. In 1881, it was for members of the Voegtly Evangelical Church *only,* the church down across from the Heinz factory, remember?" She tapped the obituary with her reading glasses. "It says here quite clearly that Maria was buried out of the First German Protestant Evangelical Church at Sixth and Smithfield. The two parishes were both congregational but quite different. And at odds with each other."

Dee just stared. "So where is she, then? The obituary says she was buried in Troy Hill. There's got to be another cemetery up here."

"Well," Ms. Seltsham said tartly, "there isn't." And then she added, softening a little, "At least not anymore, there isn't."

"There was once, though?" Dee asked, sitting up.

"Oh, yes, indeed." Ms. Seltsham nodded. "Maria, as her obituary says, was buried in what was known as the Troy Hill Cemetery. It was owned by Smithfield Church, obviously Maria's parish, since she was buried out of it. *That* Cemetery was at the other end of town, right where Lowrie dead-ends into Gardiner, but it's been gone for over a hundred years."

Ms. Seltsham glanced at Dee and smiled, apparently at Dee's expression. "No. That does *not* mean Maria is buried under asphalt—not if she had any family in the area who cared about her."

"I think she did," Dee said.

"Then almost certainly they moved her remains," Ms. Seltsham said without hesitation. "That is, they paid to have it done." She slid her rain-soaked shawl off her head and down around her shoulders. Her hair was glossy black, Dee saw, and was pulled back tight and looped into a complicated knot at the nape of her neck. There was not a white strand in it.

"You see," Ms. Seltsham went on, warming to her

subject, "somewhere toward the end of the century, the church closed its cemetery up here and sold the land to the town. It was almost full anyway and had always been inconvenient for parishioners who had to come up here from center city. So the church purchased another cemetery, Smithfield Cemetery out in Squirrel Hill, and closed this one."

"I know Smithfield Cemetery. I've been all through it."

"Listen," Ms. Seltsham said, holding up one finger, reminding Dee of Jury. "Now, the closing of a cemetery is not an overnight matter. You have to give public notice of it and then offer all the families of all the people buried there the opportunity to have their relatives' remains moved. Of course, the families had to bear the expense of this—the exhumation, the transfer of the remains—and they had to pay for a new headstone too, if they chose to have one. Usually plots in the new location were free because all the other expenses were quite high."

"Ms. Seltsham," Dee interrupted, unable to contain herself. "I don't think Maria's in Smithfield Cemetery. I've checked every gravestone in there. I mean, I checked those graves stone by stone. And I checked the church records too. I know where every Dietrich in there is, just like you know where they are here. There's no Maria Louisa Dietrich buried in Smithfield Cemetery."

Ms. Seltsham stared at her for a moment. "But headstones are no guide as to who is buried in a cemetery—

unless, of course, there was a cemetery policy requiring them, as there is at Voegtly. Does Smithfield Cemetery have such a policy, do you know?"

"I don't think so. There are a lot of unmarked graves there."

Ms. Seltsham nodded. "Twenty to thirty percent of the bodies in most old cemeteries are in unmarked graves, and even church records can be misleading about who's where, unless you know history."

Suddenly, as suddenly as if someone had turned off a tap, the rain stopped. The only sound was a gurgling of water, as though they were parked by a brook.

"I'm sorry I interrupted," Dee said. "Please, go on about . . . how the cemeteries worked."

"I'm just trying to reconstruct what may have happened," Ms. Seltsham said.

"Of course," Dee said. "Please, take your time."

Ms. Seltsham put her reading glasses back on and looked down again at the obituary. "Your great-great-grandmother was only thirty-seven when she died. Let's say that her husband, Conrad H., was about her age, and, after a decent interval, that he married again."

Dee remembered that this was exactly what Kate's father had done, after the decent interval of only a little more than a year.

"He has a couple of children with his new wife, let's say, and maybe there are even some children from his first marriage to take care of as well. And then"—Ms.

Seltsham raised a forefinger again—"maybe a decade later, Conrad gets word from his church that the Troy Hill Cemetery is going to be closed and its land taken over by the town. If he wishes the body of his first wife moved to the church's new cemetery, Smithfield, a plot will be given him free, say, or maybe at half price. But he will have to pay for the exhuming and reburying. And if he wants a headstone, which will have to be new, chances are, because all cemeteries have their own specifications for such things, then he will have to pay for that too. What do you think someone in Conrad's situation, man or woman, with a new spouse and new children, might do? Or might be tempted to do?"

Dee gave the obvious response to Ms. Seltsham's question. "Refuse to pay, I suppose."

"Of course. And maybe that's what happened with Maria. We do have to face that as a possibility anyway."

Ms. Seltsham paused, and Dee asked, "What did they do with the remains of people whose families wouldn't pay to have them . . . relocated?"

"Just let them lie. They found some skulls over on Gardiner Street a couple of years ago when they had to dig up the street for something or other. Everybody around here was terribly upset."

Damn! Dee thought, leaning her head against her side window. Kate's mother probably *was* buried under asphalt.

"However," Ms. Seltsham continued, "it's not likely

that Conrad just left Maria's body where it was. Closing a cemetery takes a couple of years, and as I say, it's a very public event; all the names are published in the newspapers and that sort of thing. Whatever Conrad decided to do about his wife's remains, in other words, was open to public scrutiny, so chances are that out of decency he at least paid to have Maria exhumed and reburied—or if he couldn't afford it, that some other member of her family did."

"Yes," Dee said, sitting up again, "I can see that."

"But it's easy to see how Conrad might have drawn the line at buying a new headstone. They were expensive, for one thing, and he'd probably already paid for one. For another, second wives, or husbands, are likely to be a bit . . . sensitive about that kind of ongoing loyalty to an earlier spouse."

"I can see that too, but if . . . if Maria is just lying in an unmarked grave somewhere in Smithfield Cemetery, a grave that not even the church has a record of, how am I supposed to find her?"

"It's not, if you will forgive me," Ms. Seltsham said archly, "a question of what you are 'supposed' to do. Maria may be in an unmarked grave, but that does not mean there's no way of finding it. The church has no record of her having been *buried* at Smithfield, because technically she wasn't. She was *re*buried there. And in a lot of churches, particularly old ones, such records are kept separate from burial records. Did you think to ask at Smithfield whether they had a Book of Reinterments or some such and have them check in there for Maria?"

Dee hadn't, of course, and her heart leaped with hope. She rolled down the window on her side of the car and breathed in deeply. It was as though the whole world had been newly mowed. She laughed. "What a dunce you must think I am. Of course I never thought to ask about a Book of Reinterments, but I can promise you I will." She checked her watch; 3:45. "I will today. If I leave now, I can probably just catch the people down at the church this afternoon, don't you think? It can't be more than twenty minutes away." She laughed again. "Ms. Seltsham, I don't know what I'd have done if I hadn't run into you. And I don't know how to thank you." She extended her hand.

Ms. Seltsham took it but with an expression Dee couldn't read. "But I thought . . . ," Ms. Seltsham said. "But I thought . . ."

There was a commotion outside the window next to Ms. Seltsham and a great drawn-out cry of indignation.

Dee smiled. "I guess Harold will be as glad to get dry as we will. I'm sorry the rain gave him such a bad time."

Ms. Seltsham opened her door and struggled out of the seat onto her feet. There were spots of red at her cheekbones. She undid the leash from the side-view mirror and, without a word, without so much as a glance in Dee's direction, headed for her house.

It stunned Dee. Obviously, she'd offended Ms. Seltsham in some way. Should she have offered to drive her home, even if it meant having Harold in the car with them?

Dee pulled the car back onto the narrow parked-up street, U-turned as quickly as she could, and drove up alongside Ms. Seltsham. It was she who hailed Dee, however, by stepping off the brick sidewalk and raising her whip.

"I'm so sorry to hold you up," she said with cold civility before Dee could say anything, "but I have one more thing to tell you. It is important that you know your relative's maiden name before you go down to Smithfield Church."

"Your relative." It was no longer "your great-great-grandmother" or "Maria." Dee really had offended her.

"Ms. Seltsham," she began, "I'm sorry if my tone—"

"When a wife's family, rather than her husband, took on the expense of moving her body," Ms. Seltsham said, riding right over Dee's attempt at an apology, "they sometimes reburied her under her maiden name. If you think about it, perhaps you can see why. And that is all I have to say to you."

Dee could feel her face flaming. "Ms. Seltsham, please," she tried again. But the old woman had already turned her back and stepped briskly away, her cat proudly in step with her, as though both of them marched to the same beat of the same different drum.

CHAPTER 17

E ven in the stop-and-go traffic of rush hour, Dee felt as though she were riding to The Colony on the crest of a wave. She would share the news with Cory first. Then she'd go to her apartment and share it with Megan. And then she'd call Harry so they could talk about how to handle things with Jury.

The last piece of the puzzle had fallen into place less than an hour ago down at Smithfield Church. Yes, the church did indeed have a Book of Reinterments, which the secretary, reminding Dee of her morning visit to Sampson's, had taken a while to bring up from the basement. Most of the book's entries were in German. There'd been no reburial listed for a Dietrich from 1889 to 1891 (the length of time it had taken Troy Hill Cemetery to close), but yes, the remains of a Maria Louisa *Hauptmann* (Dee got her maiden name from Kate's death certificate; it wasn't on Harry's data sheet) had been moved from Troy Hill to her family's plot in Smithfield on December 1, 1891. The Hauptmann family owned six graves in section C, graves 207 to 212. Maria (and therefore Kate) was in 211. There was no headstone for it, but Dee took notes on how the plot was laid out.

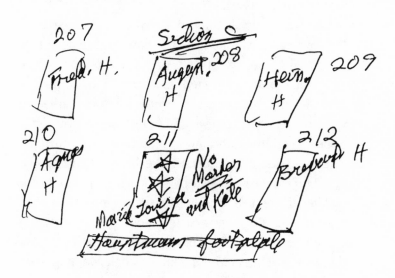

As traffic continued to inch forward, Dee felt a deep tiredness slowly seep into her, and her head began to ache. She hadn't slept much the night before. When she reached the building where Cory lived and worked, however, her excitement picked up again. She parked in the free public lot close by and, cutting across traffic, ran to the huge steel door on which "The Colony" was blazoned in fancy Gothic script. Under that was the single word POUND. Dee pounded, first with one fist, then with both. It was like hitting the side of a building, and she heard absolutely nothing in response. She turned around and began stamping on the door with the flat of her foot, more or less rhythmically.

The Colony was housed in what had once been the four-story warehouse of a now-bankrupt storage company. In the 1980s, five or six artists had moved into the long-abandoned building and begun to renovate it. Nobody had protested their takeover very much, particularly after the artists attracted some favorable national attention by covering the whole outside of the fortresslike building with cheerfully surreal designs. Two of the original members had had law degrees, and somehow they'd gotten the place chartered as a tax-free artists' co-op.

You could join The Colony only by invitation, and there were always more qualified people wanting to get in than the twenty for which it had room. It was definitely not a hangout for losers. You could be as unconventional as you liked, but no drugs or alcohol were allowed, you couldn't break the law in any way, and you worked hard and regularly at your art or you were moved out.

"Yeah," Dee heard finally from behind the door. It

was a surly voice and sounded as though it were coming from the bottom of a mine.

"I want to see Cory," she yelled.

"What?" the voice bawled, more audibly this time.

"Cory," Dee screamed. "Cory Windhover."

For a moment there was silence. Then the voice came from behind the door again. *"Who?"*

Dee resumed her stamping and, after a while, heard what sounded like swearing and then the snicking of bolts. The door opened about a foot on a Hispanic guy who looked like a biker. He had fierce red-rimmed eyes and a beard clogged with gobs of plaster. The one arm Dee could see sticking out of a cutoff sweatshirt was black with tattoos.

"I have to see Cory," she said, stepping forward. "Cory Windhover." It didn't move the biker an inch.

"Come on," she said exasperatedly. "I go with Cory, and I'm in a hurry. You must be new here."

"I'm not supposed to—"

"Help! Help!" Dee shouted through the crack of the open door. "Help me out here! I need some help!" She knew that almost everybody worked on the first floor so there were always people there.

The biker swore again and tried to close the door on Dee's sneaker. It hurt. "Ow! Ow! Ow!" she roared. "He's hurting me! He's hurting me!"

There was the sound of footsteps, more swearing, and all of a sudden the door came off Dee's foot and opened wide enough for her to see someone alongside the biker, peering out at her. It was a man she'd seen a couple of times, a painter named Mel. A nice guy with the warm good looks of a news anchor.

"God, Dee," he said to her, opening the door wide. "Cool it, will you? What's going on?"

"All I want is to see Cory," she said, stepping inside and glaring at the biker. "This bozo didn't want to let me in. Who is he, by the way? I've never seen him before."

"I didn't know who the kid was, Mel," the biker said. "She just tried to barge right in." He spoke with an accent, Dee noticed.

"It's okay, Fork," Mel said, smiling at him. "She's Cory's girl." And then he said to Dee, "Fork's new here. Pearl got married. He's a better sculptor than she was, though." Mel looked down the hall that led back from the entranceway. "If Cory isn't in his work space, he's in the lounge. Or maybe he's crashed for a while."

Most of The Colony's first floor, which was pillared like a parking garage and half the size of a football field, had been subdivided into a number of work spaces, each assigned to a particular artist. Some of the spaces were furnished quite elegantly with rugs, pictures, and expensive furniture. Others, such as Cory's, were strictly utilitarian. The place would have had a kind of egg-carton feel, with its many subdivisions, had it not been for the riotous combination of colors, shapes, and objects it contained. There were mobiles and sculptures of wrought iron, of brass, of papier-mâché. A large section of ceiling was covered with a lot of long pastel-tinted silk sheets that billowed as though they were breathing. And the walls were an eye-dizzying array of murals, graffiti-like drawings, and intricate woven tapestries. A hall ran from the entranceway past the work spaces and ended at the lounge, a kind of social center with couches, a couple of card tables, a television set, a pool table, and at one end, behind a partition, a small kitchen.

Cory wasn't in his work space, so Dee went down to the lounge. At first there didn't seem to be anybody there either, but then she heard sounds from the kitchen. "Cory!" she cried. "Wait'll you hear what I found!"

When Dee pushed open the hinged louvered doors, she saw Cory facing her, his face scarlet, his eyes wide with fear. To one side of him was Harry. She had her back to Dee and was frantically stuffing her blouse back into her skirt.

"Dee!" Cory cried. "Dee!"

She simply froze, thinking nothing, feeling nothing. Then she turned, stumbling her way from the lounge toward the front door.

"Dee!" she heard Cory cry again. "Please, wait!" But she didn't stop.

She'd almost reached the doorway of the lounge when she felt her arm taken. "Wait a minute, please,

Dee. Just wait a minute," she heard Harry say, but Dee brought the side of her free hand down on Harry's wrist as hard as she could, and then she was free. In another moment she burst out the front door of The Colony into the mockery of a freshly rain-washed world glistening with promise in the late afternoon sun.

CHAPTER 18

D ee drove through East Liberty and up into Highland Park without either direction or intent.
She stopped at a vacant parking area surrounded
by still-dripping trees and walked out past a number
of empty picnic tables to a forlorn-looking pavilion
that was also empty. How long she sat on a bench
there, staring at nothing, she had no idea.

Cory and Harry together. Cory and Harry both.

Betrayal. Her life was nothing but a series of betray-
als, and she was sick of it.

She'd go tell Jury where Kate's grave was. He could
use the information to recover the diary, and he
could do with it whatever he wanted. She was done.

At Jury's front door, Dee handed him her sketch of
the Hauptmann plot out at Smithfield Cemetery, showed

him which grave was Kate's, and then attempted to leave. But he insisted she come inside, where, seated in his living room, haltingly at first, but then in a great rush, she told him everything—all about her relationship with Harry, all of what she had learned about the disposition of Kate's body, and all, generally all, of what she'd seen at The Colony.

For the most part, Jury just sat and listened, fingers steepled, only the tips touching, his nostrils flaring slightly from time to time. He made Dee tea. He handed her Kleenex as she needed it. He asked her to clarify certain things. But mainly he listened. Finally, spent, Dee slumped back in her armchair, and all was silent for a time until an old dial phone on the end table beside Jury shrilled. He put his hand on the receiver but then hesitated. "This is almost certainly for you, Dee. Both Cory and Megan called earlier wanting to know if I knew where you were. If you don't feel like talking to either of them now, I think you should at least let them know you're all right."

"Oh, Jury," she wailed, "not now. Can't *you* just say . . . I'm okay?"

"I think you'd better be the one to say it."

Dee nodded and crossed the room. It was Megan on the phone, which Jury handed her. "I'm all right. Don't worry."

"Dee, Cory's here. He's worried sick about you."

"Tell him I don't want to see him."

"For God's sake," Megan said. "Can't you—"

"It's a long story, Megs. I'll tell you everything when I get home. I found Kate's grave, by the way, but I really mean that I don't want to see Cory or talk to him. Make him go home." She paused a moment. "You were right about Harry," she said. Then she hung up and returned to the armchair.

Dee had been in Jury's living room only two other times, the night she and Megan and Cory had had Chinese food with him and the night they'd had pizza. It was exactly the sort of setting she'd have imagined for him. Polished wood floors. Worn, elegant-looking Persian rugs. Walls of bookcases. The softly ticking grandfather clock. There were two old armchairs stuffed with something that made a scritching sound when you sat on them and a number of end tables with photographs in stand-up frames. On one end of one bookcase hung three black-and-white prints of the ruins of a temple of some sort, its tumbled-down columns laced with ivy. There was a sideboard of dark carved wood. The room glowed with integrity.

Jury rubbed his throat. "So you've been . . . reporting to Harry all along, then?"

Looking down, unable to meet his eyes, she nodded, feeling the threat of more hot tears. She blinked them back. Then she looked up quickly. "Nothing about the death certificate or about the grave though. Where it is. I didn't tell Harry about *anything* I learned today."

She paused and shook her head. "That's no credit to me, though. I would have told her everything. I was going to talk to her right after—" She stopped. "I can't *believe* I was such a fool about . . . everything."

"I know the feeling," Jury said with a curt nod. "Believe me. I know the feeling."

"People are such *liars!*" Dee cried.

"No," Jury said. "Not all people are. All people tell lies, but not all people are liars."

Dee chewed her lip. "Cory and Harry sure are a pair of liars."

"No," Jury said again. "Harry is, but Cory is not."

"Oh, really," Dee said sarcastically. "If Cory's not, then why'd he make a move on Harry?"

"He didn't. Harry made the move. At least that's what I think happened."

Dee stared at him.

"I know what I'm talking about here, Dee. When you didn't telephone her last night the way she told you to, when you just left your message on her office machine, she figured you'd found the diary, or the grave at least, and thought you were cutting her out of everything, which, believe me, my dear, is exactly what she'd have done had your positions been reversed. The move, by the way, wasn't on Cory's person. She went after what Cory knew, not him."

"You don't know that," Dee snapped at him. "Maybe Cory's been . . . getting it on with Harry all along. He said she was sexy. And she seemed to be after a little more than what Cory knew when I saw them this afternoon."

"Nonsense," Jury said. "Sheer nonsense. Ask Megan what she thinks if you don't believe me."

Dee didn't want to think about things that way. "What good would it do Harry to get to Kate's grave first anyway?" she went on. "It's only a marker to where the diary is. And you're the only one who knows how."

Jury looked at her a while with his snow leopard eyes. "The grave is not a marker in the way you think. I told Harry it was, just as I told you it was. Later, I even elaborated on the lie for Harry."

"What do you mean?"

"I told her that the diary was buried in a waterproof box five paces on a line running dead north from Kate's headstone. How deep, I told her, I didn't know. But of course none of that is true."

Again, Dee stared at him without speaking.

"The diary's in Kate's grave, Dee, where Gram buried it together with her ashes almost a hundred years ago. What Kate expected, I see now, was for Gram to pick up her ashes at Sampson's, mingle the ashes of the burned diary with them, and then deposit both in her mother's grave—that is, in the grave in Smithfield where her mother's remains had been moved. Ashes to ashes, in a manner of speaking, you see. But what Gram did was to deposit the *unburned* diary and Kate's ashes in that grave—the one you found today. I've always known that the unburned diary and Kate were . . . together—though I didn't know any of the particulars. But I never told Harry what I knew."

The tick of Jury's grandfather clock was as steady as the beating of a heart.

"I may be a very foolish, fond old man in some ways, Dee," Jury said, "but I am not an idiot. I never trusted Harry."

"Or us either, I guess," Dee said. And then she added bitterly, "With reason, in my case, of course."

Jury shifted his position. "Look, Dee," he said finally. "I want to explain something. And to do it, I'm afraid I have to go into Harry's story about my . . ."—he gestured—". . . my overtures to her. I don't mean to embarrass you, but I need to know *exactly* what Harry said I did to . . . to make advances."

Dee hesitated a moment and then told him precisely what Harry had told her, which enabled her also to tell him more specifically what she'd seen at The Colony just a couple of hours earlier.

Jury looked off again and nodded. "It almost tempts one to think she has things down to a system, doesn't it?" he said, and then he glanced at Dee and smiled ruefully.

"Only a couple of key details are off in her account

of what happened with me," he said wryly. "It was *she* who betrayed me finally, not the other way around. *I* was the one who proposed a contract, for example, but she would never sign it. She kept fussing about the wording of things—and incidentally, Dee, we have no contract with each other that would give her any claim to the diary or what's in it whatsoever. Also, it was she who called *me* to ask that I come to her apartment that night, not I who forced my way in. In fact, she said on the phone that she'd decided to sign the contract and wanted me to come pick it up. When I got there, she fixed us each a drink—to toast our collaboration, she said—in spite of my saying I didn't want one, and it was later on that . . . Dee, *she* was the one who took my hands and—and—" He didn't finish the sentence.

"Look, Jury," she said, embarrassed for him. "You don't have to—"

"Yes," he interrupted, his face flushed, "I do. It's important that you understand why I'm sure what you saw at The Colony today was a pure power play on Harry's part. Nothing more than that."

"It was a little more than that for Cory," she said tartly.

"It was for me too," Jury said. "I can admit that. But what I'm also saying is that she engineered whatever happened."

"He betrayed me."

227

"That, of course, is what Harry said about me. And what people said Kate did to her husband and children."

Afraid she was going to cry again, Dee squeezed her eyes shut and pressed the heels of her hands against her temples as hard as she could.

Jury got up. "We both need some rest," he said. "But before you go, I need to be sure of a couple of things. The Hauptmann graves: they're what you'd call easy to find as a grouping?"

Dee too got up. "They should be. Section C is almost in the middle of Smithfield, right near a mausoleum that I remember. Roth is the name on the mausoleum, and it has a stained-glass window in it of a lamb with a flag in its foot. You won't have any trouble."

"And," Jury said, picking up the sketch she'd given him from the end table by his chair, "there's no stone for Kate's grave, you said?"

Dee took the paper back and pointed to the bottom of it. "No, but she's in the only grave of the six without one."

"All right. Just one more thing. Do you have any idea, I mean, from either the plot plan you saw down at the church today or from your memory of Smithfield, whether these Hauptmann graves are in what you'd call a . . . a crowded section of the cemetery? Or are they more off by themselves?"

Dee did her best to think. Her head ached terribly.

"It seemed pretty crowded to me. On the plot plan, all the plots around those six looked filled, as I remember. Is that bad?"

"That's good," he said. "And now, Dee, you must go home so that we both can rest. I will need you here at nine o'clock tomorrow morning. You and Megan and Cory." He began to walk toward his front door. Dee at first just stood and then hurried after him.

"Wait a minute, Jury. What do you mean, 'You and Megan and Cory'? I'm out of this. I'm through with this whole thing."

Jury made a sound of irritation. He turned to her, his hand on his front doorknob.

"Are you?" he said in mock surprise. "Are you really? Did it ever occur to you that maybe this whole thing may not be through with you yet? And you are still in my employ, remember."

"Jury, I found Kate's grave for you. That was the deal."

"No," he said firmly. "The deal was to come to the aid of Katherine Dietrich Miller, if you recall the wording of my newspaper ad, and we are not finished yet. I will need your services along with those of Cory and Megan tomorrow morning, thank you very much, and not to help me dig up a grave either. I will need you for something else."

"Like what?"

"Just be here at nine sharp, please."

"Jury," Dee whined, "I can't deal with Cory tonight.

Megan's already sent him home anyway. He's probably with Harry."

"Don't talk like a fool, Dee. Cory isn't home, and he isn't with Harry. He's at your apartment with Megan waiting to talk to you."

"How do you know?"

"How do I know?!" Jury heaved a heavy sigh. "Look," he said, "if Cory *isn't* waiting for you, we won't worry about him either tonight or tomorrow. If he is, he comes along in the morning—and so do you. Fair enough?"

She didn't answer.

"Dee," Jury said, opening his front door, "I'm really very tired."

"Okay," she said. "But sometimes I think you're as manipulative as Harry is."

CHAPTER 19

Both Megan and Cory were waiting when Dee got back to the apartment.

"Will you listen to me, Dee?" Cory said, his hands, palms up, spread in front of him. "Please. All you have to do is—"

Dee shook her head and waved one hand weakly. "Not now, please," she said. "Not now." She leaned back against the apartment door and closed her eyes.

"Dee," Cory blurted out. "It was wrong. I know it was wrong, and I'm sorry. I really am. But it just . . . happened. I wasn't *planning* it, I mean. I admit I kissed her. But I wasn't trying to make a move on her or anything like that. And it didn't *mean* anything. It—"

She opened her eyes and gave him a look that stopped him cold. And then she closed her eyes again.

"See," Cory said after a time, "she called Saturday and left all these messages about a documentary she said she was thinking of doing on The Colony."

"So, of course," Dee said with her eyes still closed, "you invited her down to talk things over."

"She wanted me to come to her place. I figured The Colony would be better. She brought down all these drawings of layouts and stuff, and she talked to a whole bunch of us."

"It wasn't a whole bunch of you today," Dee said tersely. She opened her eyes and looked over at Megan. "He tell you about this afternoon with my good old colleague Harry?"

"That woman's a bitch, Dee. I told you. Do you know she pumped your man here all Saturday night and all day Sunday about Kate's grave? She was sure you'd found it and told him where it was."

Jury had been right, then, about Harry's motives, Dee thought, but she was still too hurt to just forgive and forget.

"So," she said to Cory, "Harry was at The Colony all Saturday and all Easter Sunday and all day today too, I suppose. And was today an example of just how she 'pumped' you?"

"She wasn't down at The Colony *all* those days at all. And believe it or not, Dee, I never touched her before today. Honest to God. In fact, she started it."

"I believe that," Megan said.

Dee went over to the couch, sat down, and started to cry.

Cory came over and sat down awkwardly next to her. "I'm sorry, Dee," he said. "I really, really am."

After a time, Dee pulled herself upright, and Megan, who was sitting in the chair opposite her, got up and handed her a box of Kleenex. Dee took three or four sheets, wiped her eyes, blew her nose hard, and then laughed briefly. She wadded the tissues into a ball and held it up in front of her. "I must have gone through a case of this stuff so far today. God, but I'm tired."

And then Dee began to tell them all that had happened to her. How long she talked, she had no idea.

"What's up at nine tomorrow, do you think?" Megan asked when Dee had finished. "She looked at her watch. "It's not all that far away."

"I don't know," Dee said, getting up and almost falling. "All I know is that I've got to lie down for a while." She stumbled to her room and flung herself across her bed into a dark sea of sleep.

Just before 9:00 the next morning, Dee, Megan, and Cory arrived at Jury's house to find him sitting on the top porch step waiting for them. He picked up a large manila envelope beside him, stepped briskly down to the car, and got in the front seat, but his drawn gray face didn't fit his jauntiness. His eyes were unnaturally bright, like a pair of diamonds.

"Good morning," he said first to Megan and then to Cory and Dee in the backseat. "I owe you all an apology. Last night, Dee, I'm afraid I didn't stop to consider that you and Megan might have classes today and that I was asking you to give them up just on my account. As a former teacher, I take the processes of education seriously. And, Cory, I know your work schedule. All of you, in other words, have interrupted your lives for an obsessed old man, and I'm grateful. This should not take us all that long, however."

"I wouldn't call you *old* exactly, Jury Giraffe," Megan said, grinning as she pulled away from the curb. "And what shouldn't take all that long?"

Jury pointed ahead. "Would you turn left at that next corner, please, and then left again on Highland? I'm afraid I must trouble you to stop at Young's Insurance Agency. I need to have some things notarized." He looked at his watch. "It's five past nine. Mr. Young always opens at nine o'clock sharp. This should only take a moment."

Megan looked at Cory and Dee in the rearview mirror, but Dee deliberately turned her head away. She still had a headache; lots of aspirin and even the sunglasses she wore hadn't seemed to help. Cory rubbed the back of her hand, which she was too tired to pull away.

Taking the two left turns Jury had told her to, Megan drove to Young's Insurance Agency midway down the block. Jury headed for the entrance as soon as the car had stopped, carrying his manila envelope in one hand.

Megan drummed her fingernails on the steering wheel. "Wonder what he has to get notarized," she said.

Dee looked out her side window and crossed her arms over her chest. Cory didn't say anything.

"Maybe it has something to do with taxes," Megan speculated. "Isn't it tax-paying time?"

Again, neither Dee nor Cory responded.

Jury was more like a half hour than a moment. When he finally returned to the car, the manila envelope was gone and he had several bulky white business envelopes that he put on the console between Megan and himself. "I'm sorry it took so long," he said. "There were . . . complications I hadn't foreseen." He glanced at the backseat and flashed Dee a strange smile. "From here on, the navigation is yours, my dear."

Dee leaned forward. "To the . . . cemetery?"

"Megan knows the way to the cemetery. We need you to take us to Kate's grave. You must tell us where to park. Not too near the grave, please, and so that we may walk downhill to it, if possible."

"What are those?" Megan said, looking down at the envelopes Jury had put between them.

"These," he said, picking them up and putting them into his inside coat pocket, "are birdlime."

"What's birdlime?"

He leaned toward her, winked, and gave her the

same strange smile he had given Dee. "Wait and see," he said in a hoarse stage whisper. Dee became more and more anxious. Jury wasn't the winking, smile-flashing sort.

Megan took the long winding drive off Forbes Avenue up into the center of Smithfield Cemetery. At the top of the hill, Dee told her to park, and everyone got out of the car. Although it was the same cemetery Dee had walked the grounds of less than three weeks ago, the young spring sun made it feel a brighter place, more hopeful. All the dead weeds around the ruined chapel on the hill to their left had greened, making the building itself look as though it were sprouting. Most of the wreaths and sprays of Easter flowers had been hammered to pieces by yesterday's thunderstorm, but here and there individual flowers, tossed free by the wind, still glowed in the grass like jewels. Dee felt her spirits begin to rise almost in spite of herself.

"How alive everything feels," Jury said, looking down the slope. "The grass out here really is like the beautiful uncut hair of graves, isn't it?"

"What's that?" Dee asked him.

"Just a quotation, my dear," he said. "Nothing to trouble about." He then pointed to the far corner of the cemetery. "And is that not the excellent Mr. Jerry Giraffe?"

It was, dragging an enormous black plastic trash

bag. After a while, he noticed them and let out a whoop. Dropping his bag, he came chugging in their direction.

"He looks like the Little Engine That Could," Megan said as they watched him climb.

"I know a riddle!" Jerry cried, grinning as he drew near. His hair was exactly as it had been the first time they'd seen him, a great viny tangle, most of it hanging in his face.

"I know you know a riddle," Jury said, "and a good one too. But we have work to do this morning, Jerry. You can walk with us, if you like. Have you been picking up Easter flowers, the loose ones?"

Jerry bobbed his head and pointed back downhill at several huge trash bags, all of them crammed to capacity, lying in a pile next to the cemetery office. Then he took Jury's arm and said, "Have to fix hair."

Jury looked at his watch. "Not today, Jerry. I'm afraid I don't even have a rubber band."

Jerry just looked at him. "Judge and Jury Giraffe," he said, smiling and patting Jury's chest. Then he patted his own chest. "Jerry Giraffe."

"Precisely so, Jerry," Jury said, and then he clapped his hands for attention. Jerry then clapped his.

"All right now, people," Jury said. "Will you orient us, Dee, if you please?"

She pointed to a square marble building near the bottom of the hill. A kind of aisle of grass, flanked by

graves on both sides, led down to it. "See that mausoleum down there? Kate's ashes are buried about fifteen yards or so uphill from it on the right in the only
unmarked grave in the Hauptmann family plot. There's
supposed to be a footplate."

"Thank you," Jury said to her. And then he addressed
everyone: "Now, listen carefully, please." He took a garden trowel from his inside pocket and handed it to
Cory. "I'd like us to walk together down the hill to
that partially visible footplate on the right just past
the stone cross. It's about twenty yards down. Do you
see it?"

They all did.

"At that footplate we'll stop while you, Cory, expose
it completely. When you do, we will gather together as
though deliberating. After a while, we will move on to
the next footplate on the left. Do you see it in front of
the stone obelisk? Again, Cory, you'll reveal the whole
footplate, but this time after you do, we're going to
celebrate, as though we've found a treasure."

"Like Kate's grave," Megan said, grinning. "All this
is for Harry's benefit, isn't it? In case she should be
watching?"

"Not 'in case,' Megan. She is watching, I assure
you. There isn't time for me to go into why now, but
I invited Harry to meet us out here at ten-thirty—
please *don't* look over now—by the ruined chapel.
But I'm sure she was here early and that she'll make

an appearance as soon as we engage in our mock celebration."

"The man with a plan," Megan said, grinning again. "You are one cool dude, Jury Giraffe."

"Judge and Jury Giraffe," Jerry said solemnly.

"What do we do when she shows up?" Cory asked.

"Just follow my lead. I have a surprise for her," Jury said, checking his watch again. "I think we'd better start down." His face still looked taut to Dee, his cheerfulness forced.

"The surprise you have," Megan asked him, "is that the birdlime?"

"Yes," he said. "Not the best quality birdlime, I'm afraid, but the best I could do with only one night's preparation."

As the five of them made their way carefully down past the rows of neatly tended graves, Dee saw that Cory was walking close alongside Jury, ready to take his arm if he needed it.

As soon as they reached the first footplate Jury had pointed out, Cory went over with the trowel, dropped to his knees, and carefully exposed the whole of it. "Himmel," he announced.

"Very well," Jury said. "Just stay where you are, Cory. Ladies," he said to Dee and Megan, "come closer to me, as though we were talking something over. I will recite something to you, and then you can react to it."

It was a poem. "'That time of year thou mayest in me behold,'" Jury began, "'Where yellow leaves or none or few do shake against the cold.'"

"That's Shakespeare," Dee said when he'd finished.

"It is," Jury said, nodding. "Now let's go down to the next footplate."

When they stood alongside it, Cory again cleaned it off. "Schmidt-Drang," he said.

Jury gave a shout. "Yes," he cried out. "Yes. Yes."

"Yes. Yes," Jerry cried from close by Jury's side.

"We've got her," Cory called out to Megan, who had gone a few steps farther down the hill but came running back. There was still no one in sight that Dee could see.

The Schmidt-Drang grouping contained twelve graves, three rows of four. Five had no markers. Jury went to one of these, the second from the right in the top row, and pointed down. "Right here," he said in a loud voice.

"Here," Jerry echoed. Then, in a lower voice, Jury instructed Dee, Megan, and Cory to stand in a circle with him and hold hands. Jerry of course came with them. "Just follow my lead, remember, and be patient."

They joined hands. Jerry smelled to Dee very much like the turned earth in her mother's garden and she thought also of Cory's hands. "Please bow your heads," Jury said, and then he spoke in Latin: "*Magna est veritas et praevalebit.*"

"Mobba worry us praydababit," Jerry said, grinning, and for several moments they stood silently together in the soft sighing wind. Suddenly, from above their heads, there was a shrill whistle, and all five of them looked to the top of the slope. It was Harry, unmistakably Harry, at the crest of the hill, hands on hips, booted legs planted as though she were astride a beaten enemy. Her long dark hair was loose and streaming in the wind, and a midnight blue cape billowed up around her like a pair of wings.

"My God," Megan said. "She looks like she thinks she owns the world."

"Yes," Jury said. "That's exactly what she thinks."

Harry began working her way down the slope, the high heels of her long boots obviously giving her trouble. Once she stumbled and almost fell, at which Megan giggled. Her footsteps made a sucking sound in the rain-softened ground. By the time she got to them, both her beautiful leather boots and her cloak were splattered with mud. Jerry backed away, his eyes wide. Dee had never seen Harry in full sunshine before. Her makeup seemed like the mask of a character in a Japanese play.

"I thought we were to meet by the chapel at ten-thirty," Harry said to Jury, ignoring everyone else.

"At ten-thirty," he replied, "we'd have been there."

"Sure," Harry said sarcastically as she moved from the footplate up to check all the headstones in the grouping. "And what are we doing meanwhile? Hoping to raise Kate from the dead?"

She came back down to stand in front of Jury again. Beneath her midnight blue cape, Dee could see Harry had on a beautiful, close-fitting scarlet suit.

"I know you've either got the diary or know where it is, thanks to Miss Angel Face here, so what's the deal?"

"What do you mean, 'deal'?"

"What do you mean what do I mean? I spent a lot of time researching the Katherine Soffel case, and it was my story on it that brought you out of the woodwork. I also spent a lot of time helping you and a lot of time training that one"—she nodded in Dee's direction without looking at her—"to keep her from falling over her own feet."

"Training me?" Dee cried. *"Training me."*

"I'm entitled to a share in that diary," Harry continued, still talking only to Jury, "and you know it. So what's your proposition?"

"Talk about chutzpah!" Megan exclaimed. "I can't believe this woman."

"You don't want a *share* of the diary," Dee said to Harry. "You want it all. You never intended to give Jury anything—or me either. All your talk about being colleagues! You're nothing but a thief, Harry."

"Me?" Harry cried, clapping a hand to her chest. "*Me?* You're the thief—and after all I did for you too, you backstabbing little Judas. And now, just because your boyfriend hit on me, you're trying to cut me out of everything."

"I didn't, though!" Cory cried. "Not like that!"

"*He* hit on *you*?" Megan laughed. "Give us a break, will you, Harry?"

"All you'd have had to do was play it straight with me," Dee said to her. "That's all you'd have had to do."

"Yeah, sure," Harry said derisively. "The way you did, and Jury did, and Megan did. How straight did all of you play it with me?"

"I did, though, Harry," Dee protested. She felt her head beginning to spin, and she sat down on the edge of a headstone. "I trusted you. I really cared about you."

"Yadda, yadda, yadda," Harry sneered. Then she whirled on Jury and again pointed a finger at him. "You'd better keep in mind that this kid signed a contract with me, a legal contract, and if the two of you try to do anything with that diary that I don't have a say in, I'll sue your asses off."

"I think," Jury said with iron control, "that we have heard enough rubbish from you this morning. And if I may now have a moment of your obviously very valuable time, perhaps you would like to hear what it is I brought you out to Smithfield to say in front of witnesses."

Harry's face twitched and jerked, but she put her hands back on her hips and held her tongue.

"Very well, then," Jury said. "First, you have no right whatsoever to *any*thing connected with Kate's diary, legal or otherwise; as Kate's only known heir, I am the sole owner of the diary. That's the first thing.

"Second, the agreement you had Dee sign when you manipulated her into working for you—I believe you have still not given her a copy of it—is a standard waiver signed only by people *employed* by WHGH, which Dee never was. She was, however, in *my* employ, and I have the cancelled checks to prove it. Have you any cancelled checks?"

Dee felt the skin on her neck prickle. Jury had never given her a check.

Harry's tongue flicked out quickly to touch her upper lip. "She was to have half of everything. That was our understanding. I agreed to give her half of everything."

"Oh, Harry!" Dee exclaimed. "You never said anything about half of anything!"

"So you have no receipts of any kind, then?" Jury said dryly. "I thought not." He took out one of the envelopes he'd put in his breast pocket and handed it to Harry. "And this is the third thing, a *real* legal document, a copy—duly notarized, you will see—of my assignment of *all* the rights my grandmother gave me in Kate's diary to Dee and Cory and Megan."

Harry tore the envelope open and devoured its contents, flipping several times back and forth between pages.

"And," Jury said, after giving her time to get a sense of what he'd handed her, "you will notice that in the document I also make it clear I authorized Dee to send for Kate's death certificate."

Harry barked a laugh. "That doesn't mean anything. She had to lie about who she was to get it, and that's a crime. A felony. They'll have her name on file, and I can see to it that that kid ends up with the felony on her record. And if I don't get some rights to Kate's diary, by God, I will."

"Really?" Jury laughed. "*Really?* Even if Dee had gotten the copy of the death certificate by suggesting she was one of Kate's descendants, that would not have been a felony. A misdemeanor, yes, but not a felony. I am assured of this, incidentally, by my friend Vernon Young, attorney at law, who has notarized the document you are holding. In addition, Dee's explanations of her experience with you, along with my own, both of which will be on file with the excellent Mr. Young, and both of which will be sent immediately to your employer and to the Pittsburgh newspapers should it become necessary—these things, I think, and Mr. Young thinks as well, just might be considered by the court to be mitigating circumstances for a mere misdemeanor. What *you* might be charged with, on the other hand, and how your employer might evaluate your conduct in all this—these are different matters altogether."

Jury smiled politely at Harry and then asked her, "What do you think?"

At first Harry said nothing, her face working as though she were undergoing some kind of transformation. "So I am to have nothing, then, is that it? Well, we'll just see about that."

"Yes. Indeed we shall," Jury replied. "Mr. Young told me to tell you we'd be happy to see you in court. Now, begone, vile *Arachnida. Lusisti satis.*"

Harry crumpled the pages she was holding and threw them in Jury's face. Then she spat on the ground in front of him, whereupon Jerry scuttled down to hide behind the mausoleum.

"Hey," Megan yelled at her, "that's class, Harry. You're a real class act, you know that? Sing us a farewell aria too, why not?"

"Noli nos tangere," Jury said in a great voice. "Begone, I say."

After slogging up the hill, Harry turned as though she were about to hurl down a thunderbolt. "I promise you all—," she began, but Megan cut her off.

"I don't know how to say it in Latin exactly," Megan called, "but if you *can't* sing us a farewell aria, then how about you show us your boobs?"

CHAPTER 20

The moment Harry vanished over the crest of the hill, Jury sat down on the edge of a couch grave in the second row of the Schmidt-Drang plot. The authority with which he had dealt with Harry was leaving him like air from a balloon.

"I feel," he said, "like an exorcist who's had to work overtime. I'd like to sit for a moment and then, once we're sure she's left, go to pay my respects to Kate."

Jerry, Dee noticed, was watching them from around the corner of the mausoleum.

"Come on up, Jerry," she called. "She's gone."

Looking anxiously around him, he lumbered up. "Mad lady," he said.

"And how," Megan agreed. "She looked like that queen in the Snow White movie." She then came over, sat down next to Jury, and hugged him quickly around the shoulders with one arm. "You're the man," she said.

"A tired man now"—he nodded toward the balled-up pages that Harry had thrown in his face—"from putting that together, for one thing. I was up all night. Be sure not to leave it here, by the way. I can't see her returning right away, but she may. In any event, she will certainly figure out quickly enough that it was a mistake to have walked away empty-handed."

Dee picked up the ball of paper and went over to sit on Jury's other side. There was sweat on his forehead, she noticed. "Are you all right?" she asked.

"Oh, yes," he said, smiling, but Dee could see it was with an effort. "I hope you'll forgive me for not just tumbling down to die as I would in a cheap novel."

"Don't joke about it," she said.

"Just give him a minute to catch his breath, Dee," Cory put in, and for a while no one spoke.

After a time, Cory took the ball of paper from Dee and bounced it in his hands. "Is this really a legal document?" he asked Jury, bouncing the ball back to Dee.

"Well," Jury said with a smile, "Mr. Young made it clear to me, *quite* clear, that all his notary seal testified to was that my signature was my signature." He took out a handkerchief and wiped his face.

"So it's all smoke, then?" Megan said. "Like Harry's contract with Dee?"

Jury thought for a minute. "Yes and no," he said. "I

couldn't go into court with it and come out with very much, if that's what you mean, and Harry probably suspects as much. But she wouldn't take a legal route to anything with us anyway. She has no intention of having Dee charged with a misdemeanor. What she fears is our going to WHGH and the newspapers with our stories about our experiences with her. Bad publicity. It could ruin her, and she knows it."

He took some envelopes from his inside breast pocket and handed them to Megan and Cory.

"Here are copies of what I gave the *Arachnida,* the Spider, as you call her, Megan. It's a straw document, but it's not quite smoke. It was an important step for me on the way to the real thing. I want to compliment you all, by the way, on your capital performances in our . . . exorcism—and incidentally, Megan, the Latin phrasing of your crudity would be something like *'ostende tuas mammas.'*"

They all grinned.

On her thigh, Dee had smoothed out the pages of the document Harry had crumpled up, but she hadn't made any attempt to read it. Neither Cory nor Megan had opened their envelopes. "How is this a step on the way to the real thing?" Dee asked, gesturing with what she'd smoothed out. "What's the real thing?"

Jury looked at her for a while without saying anything. "The real thing is a document Mr. Young is now preparing for the four of us to consider together."

Dee and Cory and Megan looked at one another.

"So what's the excellent Mr. Young—" Megan began, but Jury rose, stopping her. He looked at his watch.

"Now that Harry has left, I'd be grateful to you all if you'd accompany me down to Kate's grave. Afterward, we'll talk about our plans for the future."

As they walked slowly down the hill, Cory asked, "How can you be sure Harry's gone?"

Jury chuckled. "Because she imagines that at eleven-thirty this morning, she has an appointment to interview three female smoke jumpers from Vermont in her office."

Megan laughed. "Didn't I say he was the man?"

"Well," Jury said, "I wanted her out of things as quickly as possible, though my meanness of spirit in making sure she'd be all dressed up when I knew the ground out here was going to be muddy depresses me."

"But couldn't she still have someone watching us?" Cory persisted. "She didn't give that whistle."

"She could and probably does, but all she'll get out of it is more graves to have to consider than anyone could possibly deal with. Harry's worked out, you see, that Gram had to have hidden the diary out here so that it would be well concealed but relatively easy to retrieve. Burying it not very far under the surface of either Kate's grave or one adjacent to it is the most logical thing for her to have done. That way, the diary might be recovered by someone pretending to plant flowers, say, without attracting attention.

"How many grave sites does that give Harry to have to consider?" Jury went on. "There were—let me see—four graves in that first plot we stopped at, twelve in the second, and Dee says there are six graves in the Hauptmann plot. Some are marked, some are not, but since none of them has any obvious connection with Kate, Harry can't afford to discount even those with headstones."

"That's twenty-two graves," Megan said. "If the diary's in an adjacent grave, it's at least four times that many."

"That's really cool, Jury," Cory said admiringly.

"So this," Megan asked, holding up the envelope Jury had given her, "was the birdlime, right?"

"More precisely, Megan, it's what Horace would call *splendide mendax*."

"How would Horace say it in English?"

"Lying in an honorable cause."

The arrangement of the six graves in the Hauptmann plot was exactly as Dee's sketch suggested: three Hauptmanns were buried alongside one another in the top row, Friedrich, Augustus, and Heinrich, all plainly marked with reddish brown upright stones. In the lower row, the two outside graves had headstones, Agnes Hauptmann and Brevard Hauptmann. The middle grave was nothing but grass, and just under it ran a partially exposed footplate about three feet long. Cory knelt and once again began scraping back grass and dirt with the trowel. Suddenly he stopped.

"Wait a minute. There's something else here too."

Sure enough, just above the middle of the footplate but set about two inches lower in the ground was a piece of polished stone. Cory bent the turf up and away from what looked like a large smooth cobblestone, about the size of a loaf of bread.

Jury bent down, his hands on his knees, to look at it. "That's carving, isn't it? Can you clear it off any more?"

Dee knelt alongside Cory, and the two of them scrubbed at the top of the stone with wads of grass.

"Yes," Dee said. "It is carving. Numbers. I think it's a date. It ends in zero nine, the year Kate died."

And then the first two numbers on the stone were revealed very clearly: there was a three and a five that preceded the zero and the nine. The date was March 5, 1909.

Dee looked up at Jury with a stricken expression. Kate had died on August 30, 1909. The stone should have read: 8 30 09.

"There's a capital A under the date," Cory said. "Does that mean anything?"

"Jury!" Dee cried. "I *know* this is where Kate's mother was reburied. Kate's ashes *have* to be here. I don't know why the stone is wrong."

Jury sank to his knees between Dee and Cory and traced the carved numbers with his fingers. Cory and Dee looked at each other helplessly.

Then Megan, who was standing behind the three of them, snapped her fingers. "Wait a minute, people. That's not a date. It's a number. Three five zero nine A. I'm pretty sure that was Kate's prison number. Remember, Dee? It was on that data sheet Harry gave you."

"Of course," Jury cried. "The capital A means A range. It was a section of the prison."

"But why would they have put Kate's prison number on her gravestone?" Cory asked.

"Not they. She. I'm sure she insisted on it," Jury said. "Some notion of penance, I think, but who knows? The poor child. Who knows?"

Impulsively, Dee hugged Megan around the knees. "Thank God for your head for figures, Megs. I'd never have remembered."

"Bless you, Megan," Jury said to her. And then still on his knees, he said, "Just give me a moment here, if you will," and he bowed his head.

Dee and Cory rose and stepped back to stand with Megan. After a while, Jury began to chant softly in Latin:

"funeris heu tibi causa fui? per sidera iuro,
per superos et si qua fides tellure sub ima est,

invitus, regina, tuo de litore cessi.
sed me iussa deum, quae nunc has ire per umbras,
per loca senta situ congunt noctemque profundam,
imperiis egere suis; nec credere quivi
hunc tantum tibi me discessu ferre dolorem.
siste gradum teque aspectu ne subtrahe nostro.
quem fugis? extremum fato quod te adloquor hoc est."

When he seemed finished, Cory came forward to help him to his feet. "Do you want me to sort of poke around here with the trowel?" he asked. "Like I was going to plant some flowers?"

"No," Jury said. "That's something I want us to talk about first."

"Was the Latin something . . . from church?" Dee asked.

Jury looked off. "The lines are from Virgil. From the *Aeneid.* Do any of you know the poem?"

"I've read some sections," Dee said. "Translated, of course."

Jury nodded. "I was quoting Aeneas's lines to Dido, the queen who killed herself for love of him. He meets her spirit in the underworld, and . . . he tries to explain why he left her."

"Didn't he love her?" Megan asked.

Jury sighed. "Oh, yes. But he'd . . . he'd deserted her. In a way, he'd deserted her. And in those lines he tries to explain why. The gods were the ones responsible, he says, because they'd chosen him to fulfill a special destiny."

"Was that true?"

Jury didn't answer for a time. And then he said, "From one point of view, yes. Aeneas founded Rome. But he left Dido because . . . because he was Aeneas, really."

"So does she say she understands?" Megan asked. "Does she forgive him?"

Jury looked over at the ruined chapel. He shook his head. "No. She turns away. She says she wants nothing to do with him."

Dee and Cory and Megan glanced quickly at one another.

"But why did you speak those lines to Kate?" Dee asked. "You didn't desert *her.*"

Jury rubbed his forehead. "Yes," he said, "I did. There are all kinds of ways people can abandon people. Like Aeneas, I had my reasons, of course, but that's part of Virgil's point, isn't it? There are always reasons for betrayal."

"I think I understand that," Dee said after a time.

And then Cory said, "I think I do too."

Jury looked to the top of the slope where they'd parked. "I don't think I'll try climbing this hill right now," he said. "Perhaps the three of you would go get the car and drive down to the back of this mausoleum, where the excellent Jerry Giraffe and I will await you. I'd like to sit down again, I think."

"I'll stay with you," Dee said.

"No. Thank you, Dee, but I'd like a little time alone. Do be sure, please, to leave all those grave sites we stopped at as undisturbed looking as possible. Cover even the footplates again so that they're just the way they were. And be particularly sure to cover up the marker with Kate's prison number on it."

When the three returned with the car, Jerry went to the open window on the driver's side and, looking at Megan's braid, said, "Have to fix hair."

"Okay, Jerry Giraffe," she said, taking off the ties on her braid and shaking out her hair. "Wait there. I'll fix your hair."

She got out, went to Jerry, and turned him so his back was to her. From a destroyed flower arrangement just by her feet, she took a small red carnation and broke off most of the stem. "Would you like me to braid this flower in your hair?" she asked.

Jerry smiled his toothless smile.

Holding the flower in her teeth, Megan braided his hair and then fastened the carnation into the end of it. As he had with Jury, Jerry swung the braid delightedly, first to one side of his face and then to the other. Megan put her fists on her hips and nodded. Then she went around the car to open the front door for Jury, and when he was in, she went back around and got in behind the wheel.

"You do a nice tight braid too," Dee said, smiling at her.

For a while the four of them just sat, Jury and Megan in the front seat, Cory and Dee in back.

"Is this," Dee finally asked, "a good time for you to tell us about the document you said Mr. Young was writing, the real thing?"

Jury took a deep breath, as though preparing himself for an exertion. "The real thing is a contract, one I hope all four of us are going to enter into on Saturday morning at his office. It gives each of us an equal share in Kate's diary, should we decide to try to retrieve it, which is the first thing we'll have to discuss, by the way—whether, in violation of what we know were Kate's final wishes, we think we have the right to unearth her diary anyway. If we decide to do that, then we'll have to decide what to do with the diary, assuming, of course, that it's still legible after being underground for a century. All our votes will be by secret ballot, and taking any kind of action with the diary will require our unanimous approval."

"So," Megan said, "if we dig up the diary and it's readable, and if you three want to give it to the *Pittsburgh Post-Gazette,* say, and I don't—"

"Then we don't. Precisely," Jury finished.

"And you guys won't even know I was the one who put in the blackball?"

"Exactly."

No one spoke for a while.

"Why are you doing this?" Dee asked.

"Because it's the best way I can think of to protect Kate from being abandoned the way I abandoned her."

Dee leaned forward and took hold of the back of Jury's seat with both hands. "I don't see why you say you 'abandoned' Kate. How did you abandon her?"

For what seemed a long time, Jury didn't say anything.

"It's a fair question," he said finally, "but I have to go into more of my life than I'm used to talking about to answer it, and even then, I'm not sure . . ."

He half turned in his seat so that he could look at the three of them.

"My mother, Gram's daughter—Honor was her name—got pregnant with me when she was fifteen. She was unmarried and would never say who fathered me. I was . . . *filius nullius*, literally the son of nobody, a bastard, as it was known in those days. Shortly after having me, my mother left—no, she was driven from—her home, went over to the North Side, and hanged herself. It was my grandfather who abandoned her, really, but since I never knew him, for years I blamed Gram for not protecting her more, for not loving my mother enough, or the right way, or . . . or something. Anyway, when Gram made me promise what she did, I was in no hurry to try to clear the name of some half sister of someone who hadn't loved her own daughter well enough to keep her from being thrown out of her

258

home and killing herself. I told myself that the story of Kate's innocence was nonsense anyway, that the diary was no more than the fantasy of a woman deranged by the consequences of what she'd done.

"But then, last year, right after I'd retired, I was cleaning out one of Gram's trunks in the attic, and I found a letter written to her by Kate's youngest child, Clarence, in 1921, which was the year my mother was pregnant with me. Evidently, Gram, who had no money of her own, had written all four of Kate's children telling them about Honor and asking them to please send whatever they could afford to help her get started in another town somewhere, because my grandfather, though he'd taken me from my mother to raise me 'decently,' refused either to allow his daughter to live in his house or to provide for her.

"I can still remember the letter from Clarence, who wouldn't send Gram anything, of course, but who concluded by saying he was sorry to see that Kate's romantic self-indulgence, which had brought him and his family so much pain and humiliation, seemed not to have died with her."

"What a—!" Megan started, but then she stopped herself. "Well, you all know what I'd call him," she added quickly.

"At any rate," Jury said, "perhaps you can see why, from the moment I read that letter, I became Gram's champion—and vowed I would make the Soffels pay, even if in absentia, for what they'd done, for what they are."

He then turned around again and looked out the front windshield.

"There's a way, you see, in which Kate never mattered to me at all." He took a deep breath and then sighed it out again. "Regardless, when I realized that last night—about four in the morning it was actually— I wrote out the document you all have copies of, the same one I showed Harry. It assigns all the rights in the diary to the three of you. I cut myself out of everything because I was undeserving."

He sniffed a brief laugh. "About five in the morning, I saw what was wrong with what I was doing, but I left the document as I'd written it, partly because I was too tired to write another and partly because for me to seem to be giving *all* legal rights to you three looked like the best way of getting rid of Harry, which I very much wanted to do. So this morning, Mr. Young and I worked out what I believe to be a better alternative."

He paused and cocked his head, as though appraising what he'd said. Then he turned again in his seat. "I think our working together is the best chance we have of . . . of not deserting Kate, of seeing this matter through decently. We've all, for better or for worse, created a relationship with her—and with one another regarding her. We all have certain strengths,

I think—potential strengths anyway—that could make us, well, good checks and balances on one another. We're better working together, in other words, than any of us would be working alone. At least that's how I see it."

For a long time, no one said anything. And then Dee leaned forward and kissed Jury's cheek. "You're asking us to be your colleagues, aren't you? And friends? That's what the real thing is, isn't it?"

"Yes," Jury said, smiling at her. "Yes, I am. And, yes, it is."

Author's Note

This novel is based on a series of events that actually took place in Pittsburgh, Pennsylvania, at the beginning of the twentieth century. To write it, I consulted a wide variety of research material: a number of published histories and sociological studies of Pittsburgh at the turn of the century; contemporary newspaper accounts of the Soffel-Biddle case; birth, death, and burial records; church documents; diaries and correspondences of various sorts; interviews and interpretations; etc. So far as historical record exists, I have tried to find it and, in most cases, have adhered to it.

I have been asked a number of times whether, in any instance, I violate the facts of the case as they are generally understood in order to make more credible the speculations of *Compass in the Blood.* My answer is that, to my knowledge, I do not. Readers must remember, of course, that all history is fundamentally a work of the imagination and that, as the novelist Thomas Mallon says, in the phrase "historical fiction" the noun always trumps the adjective. Also, much about the Soffel-Biddle case still is simply not known, and I take advantage of this in my inferences, suppositions, and inventions.

In one respect, however, I have deliberately, and I hope successfully, misled my readers. I have scrambled what would make it possible for anyone else to locate the grave of Katherine Soffel. She did not want her final resting place marked or known. Indeed, in spite of looking for her grave for months, I found it only with the help of information from a source I am pledged not to reveal, and then by sheer accident. It is an accident I have done my best to make sure will never happen again. *Requiescat in pace.*

William E. Coles Jr.
Pittsburgh, PA